"Change. It's the one universal thing that everyone goes through, especially in high school. *Changers Book One: Drew* ratchets that up a notch and kicks open the door, with both humor and panache. Big questions and equally big highs (laughs) and lows (cries). And you thought high school was awkward before!"

—Kimberly Pauley, author of *Sucks to Be Me*

"Humor makes *Changers* a joy to read, and Drew the kind of character you'd want to be friends with in real life. I loved this book."

—Arin Greenwood, author of *Save the Enemy*

Praise for *Changers Book Two: Oryon*

"An excellent sequel . . . This installment raises the stakes, making the story not just about physical and emotional transformation, but about survival."
—*School Library Journal*

"Oryon's winning and witty narrative voice is consistently engaging . . . Oryon is African-American, and much of what he observes is about race . . . raises thought-provoking questions."
—*Kirkus Reviews*

"Addicting . . . as soon as I started reading I was immersed into the book, unable to put it down . . . The series is just getting better and better."
—*I'd So Rather Be Reading*

Praise for *Changers Book Three: Kim*

"This series takes the ultimate teen experience—not feeling comfortable in one's own skin—and folds it into a fantastical premise . . . This strong entry in the series is a good choice for readers looking for books about friendship, identity, and LGBTQ issues."
—*School Library Journal*

"Kim's voice and the banter between characters are funny, and they feel real. The identity and marginalization issues loom large, but instead of being shoehorned into side characters, they're scooped up and taken into a deeper, entertaining, fantastic narrative."
—*Kirkus Reviews*

CHANGERS

BOOK FOUR: FOREVER

CHANGERS

BOOK FOUR: FOREVER

BY T COOPER & ALLISON GLOCK-COOPER

BLACK SHEEP

This is a work of fiction. All names, characters, places, and incidents are the product of the authors' imaginations. Any resemblance to real events or persons, living or dead, is entirely coincidental.

Published by Akashic Books
©2018 T Cooper and Allison Glock-Cooper

Paperback ISBN: 978-1-61775-528-6
Hardcover ISBN: 978-1-61775-677-1
Library of Congress Control Number: 2018931796

Black Sheep/Akashic Books
Brooklyn, New York
Ballydehob, Co. Cork, Ireland
Twitter: @AkashicBooks
Facebook: AkashicBooks
E-mail: info@akashicbooks.com
Website: www.akashicbooks.com

More books for young readers from Black Sheep

Changers Book One: Drew
by T Cooper & Allison Glock-Cooper

Changers Book Two: Oryon
by T Cooper & Allison Glock-Cooper

Changers Book Three: Kim
by T Cooper & Allison Glock-Cooper

Broken Circle
by J.L. Powers & M.A. Powers

Game World
by C.J. Farley

Pills and Starships
by Lydia Millet

The Shark Curtain
by Chris Scofield

For Mary Gonzalez
1933–2016

Before he became the one he was meant to be, before he lived through those four years called high school, those four years where everything he ever knew evaporated into air, where the ground dropped away, and he fell in love, and he lived through hate and violence and the loss of his best friend, and saved lives without even knowing how, and was rescued by a girl and a boy and words and music, and he did everything wrong until he got a few important things right, before he questioned what it meant to be special, what it meant to be anything, and harnessed his power, the power he didn't believe he had, the power others tried to take, before that and a hundred other awful, wondrous, ruinous, magical things, he was just a girl in Tennessee named Kim.

SPRING

KIM

CHANGE 3-DAY 201

I lit the match today.

I lit the match and I held the flame to the dynamite and I watched the fuse burn into dust and I stood very still when the explosion went off and blew everything in my life wide open in a blinding light.

It was glorious.

Do you have any idea how amazing it feels to show people who you are?

It's like watching those Planet Earth nature specials, where every creature, every insect, every leaf, every droplet of water is so full of beauty and essential goodness that your heart buoys and your endorphins flood their happy juices, and you believe anew that the world, filled with garbage and garbage people though it may be, is still a ceaseless miracle.

That's what telling the truth about yourself feels like. Especially when you've spent years holding in a giant secret about who you are. It's like nothing so much as being born, released from darkness, exploding like a GD Katy Perry firework across the sky.

This afternoon, I was a firework. And I know there will be fallout. Debris. Cleanup. But I'm too tired to think about that. Right now I want to bask in my shine.

KIM

CHANGE 3–DAY 202

Okay, so.

Audrey knows.

Everything.

Well, not *everything*. But she knows about me. About all the me's. Or at least that there *are* multiple me's. But that they are all the same me. More or less. She'll figure the rest out. I'll help her. I'll explain, and she'll understand, and the puzzle pieces will fall into alignment, and the whole grand picture will reveal itself in all its satisfying completion. I have faith. At long last, I'm a believer!

Yesterday's RaChas visibility march devolved into a crap show of the highest order after Audrey spotted me wearing the one-of-a-kind bracelet she'd given me—well, given Drew, freshman year. The same bracelet she found in Oryon's bedroom sophomore year after we had sex. I could see the recognition click in, snap like a seat belt right as she whispered, "Drew?" in a voice both frightened and relieved. (I may be projecting the *relieved* part.)

I can't remember if I nodded or smiled or shrugged or all three, but I do know that for a full minute her eyes never left mine, and it felt, finally, like old times, when we were best friends who counted on each other more than anyone else in the world.

Audrey began to shake, and I felt the urge to embrace her, but of course, before I could, I spotted her brother tramping toward us, his puka choker straining against the engorged veins lining his neck. Jason was not having any part of the "Change is not strange!" message we were proclaiming in the streets, much less his sister rubbing elbows with any of the alterna-weirdos holding signs and screaming slogans in support of our right to be different than his version of "normal."

At his heels was Destiny (ever my protector in Chase's absence), who had stopped marching and was beelining to my side to head off Jason before he could detonate the sulfur bomb of his toxic white male privilege in my face.

As I watched Jason and Destiny both barreling our way, Audrey grabbed my forearm, flipped it over, and hooked a finger under the bracelet, getting a real good look at it. Yep, same one she gave Drew. Same one Oryon somehow had. And now Kim. She lifted her face to mine again, tears welling, as Jason and Destiny arrived at our respective sides, sandwiching Audrey and me.

"Of course, if a freak flag is waving within a hundred-mile radius, this heifer is going to show up for it," Jason barks in my direction.

"Fascist say what?" Destiny seethes, shoulder-checking Jason surprisingly hard, spinning him around.

Jason quickly recovers his balance, then laughs in Destiny's face. "You people sure are feisty," he says, licking his lips.

At that Destiny does what Destiny is going to do: she winds up and punches Jason square in the jaw so hard he falls on his ass. Audrey gasps. I glance around and notice several people filming the whole incident with their phones. I tug at Destiny's hip, pull her back.

"Walk away," I whisper. "This could get ugly."

"It already is ugly," she says, glaring at Jason, who is eye-balling her from the pavement with palpable rage.

By this time the whole Radical Changers crowd has stopped marching and chanting. Benedict has fallen oddly silent, cutting short his lecture to the TV reporter, the camera having moved on to the simmering brouhaha between Jason and Destiny. Meanwhile, Audrey is still clinging to my arm, her fingers tight around my wrist.

"Aud, I wanted to tell you," I start to mumble. "I've never *not* wanted to tell you—"

Without warning, Jason leaps up, shoving Audrey aside, launching her into the crowd as he surges toward Destiny. He reaches for Destiny's face, his hand smooshing her nose and chin like he's blocking a tackle. Behind him, Andy bursts into the melee, screaming, "Don't lay a finger on her!" and jumping onto Jason's back, the two spinning a full rotation before dropping to the ground where they begin frantically rolling and punching each other in the side of the head, the news camera trained on them the whole time.

Benedict sprints over, horrified his carefully choreo-graphed message in support of peace and embracing dif-ference has devolved into a bloody street brawl. "You're not even supposed to be here!" he yells at Andy, trying to break them up, but getting dragged into the fight himself.

Now it's the three of them—Benedict the king of the RaChas, Andy the rogue RaChas ally, and Jason the fledg-ling Abider—wrestling around on the blazing-hot asphalt, tiny rocks embedding into their elbows and knees while Destiny kicks at Jason's thighs, egging Andy on.

The few police officers who had been monitoring the march charge in, unsheathing their batons as they do. At this, Benedict extracts himself, wanting no part of the wrong side of the law (been there, done that). He bolts, expertly threading through the crowd and out of sight. The officers turn their batons on Jason and Andy, who refuse to stop fighting, the cracks of wood on bone echoing throughout the gathered crowd. After a few swings of the baton, both Andy and Jason relent, Jason yowling and grabbing his right knee in agony.

"Get up!" the cop yells at him, but Jason collapses when he tries to place any weight on his kneecap. "We don't tolerate anarchists around here."

"I'm not one of them!" Jason screams, as he and Andy are secured with plastic zip-tie handcuffs. "I have a football scholarship!"

I try to find Audrey in the chaos, finally spotting her off to one side, stunned. I jump up and down waving my arms. She sees me, starts pushing through the throng in my direction. We wade toward each other, arms outstretched. Before we connect, her mother cuts her off, snatching her by the collar of her shirt.

"Promise you'll let me explain in person!" I yell, as she is dragged backward, stumbling over bystanders. "If you never want to talk to me again after that, I'll leave you alone, I swear!"

Audrey nods her head, trying to maintain eye contact with me as her mother wrenches her farther and farther away, until I can't see her face anymore between the mass of bodies undulating in the chaos.

Beside me Destiny is hopping on the balls of her feet like a boxer who just won a bout. The few remaining Ra-Chas disperse as Jason's head is pushed into the backseat of a police car.

Andy is shoved into a different cruiser, and it hits me that I'm going to need to find a way to bail him out, with no one in town even aware of who he is, and our fearless leader Benedict bolting gods know where.

"Well, that's a sight you don't see every day," Destiny says, nodding toward the two white dudes being driven to the police station, sirens blaring. "I say we celebrate this small victory!"

I smile, but I'm distracted, unmoored. I want to celebrate my *own* small victory. I came out. And while it got messy AF, my world didn't end. On the contrary. It feels like it's finally beginning.

Here's the thing about coming clean: once you start, it's kind of hard to stop.

After I revealed myself to Audrey, I realized I had a whole long list of people I wanted to let in on my secret. This is—duh—verboten for Changers. The first rule of Changers being you don't talk about Changers. I'm sure my touchstone Tracy would want to strangle me with a canary-yellow Tory Burch belt if she found out I betrayed Changer nation. But . . . I kinda don't care anymore.

I mean, Benedict already put us all on blast. The clip of Destiny sucker-punching Jason is going viral on social media. People even started putting music to it, my favorite being the one that timed the punch to when the drums kick in on Phil Collins's "In the Air Tonight." Watching that punch land on Jason's thick head is some schadenfreude deliciousness right there. (He most def did not "feel it coming in the air," ahem.)

I'm sure the Council can't be happy about any of the exposure. Powerful as they may be, even they can't staunch the wildfire spread of Snapchat and Instagram and YouTube. There's no chapter in *The Changers Bible* about secret-keeping in the age of social media. Maybe Tracy can make an addendum with charts and graphs about how to manage the unmanageable. Charts and graphs are her reason for breathing.

Not that the exposure has amounted to that much so far. Everyone in the world is so self-obsessed these days, it barely caused a ripple in the social fabric for more than a hot second. Either people don't grasp what Changers are (likely, as Benedict intentionally encouraged vagueness in our slogans and chants), or they don't give a rat's furry butt (more likely) unless it directly interferes with or affects their own lives in some tangible way. Which brings me to Andy.

Poor, pitiful Andy. He has really gotten the booty end of the Changers stick. Falling for a Changer who left him behind, currently mooning over Destiny, as if Destiny would ever go for a guy like Andy who, let's face it, lacks swag, and not in the adorable Jon Cryer–Duckie nerdscape way. Never mind that he lost his best friend to the Changer grind too. And he had no idea. Until now.

Yeah, that's right. (See above, the part about coming clean.)

It happened after Andy and the Alt-Wrong menace that is Jason were released from jail. They were sprung mere hours after being arrested, let go with a warning about disturbing the peace. (A courtesy you can bet would never have been extended to Oryon, DJ, or Destiny, I can say from experience, and because I have, like, eyes.)

Jason's parents were already at the station, making a ruckus about his injured knee and threatening to sue the city for lost future income if he can't play football, when Destiny and I rolled up to fetch Andy. (No sign of Audrey, who was probably at home furiously googling *shape-shifters* and *genetic mutants* in hopes of figuring out what the eff Drew, Oryon, and Kim even are.)

"Looking good there, Conor McGregor," Destiny teases Andy through the open window when we spy him on the steps of the police station, spirit deflated. "I think you have some road kill on your face."

"Is that your Yubaba cosplay mask?" I add, wincing at the sight.

"Screw you both," Andy mumbles, gingerly climbing into the backseat of Destiny's car and immediately lying down flat.

"Welcome to Fight Club," Destiny says, turning to pat Andy on the knee. He huffs, pulls away.

"You should take some Advil and ice what's left of your head," I say.

"Edibles wouldn't hurt either," Destiny jokes, shifting the car into gear and peeling out past Jason climbing into his folks' black sedan, taking care to thrust her hand, middle finger extended loud and proud, out the window in his direction.

"Who even is that guy?" Andy whinges from the backseat.

"D-bag times a thousand," Destiny says.

"Hair gel in human form," I say.

"Walking abstinence advertisement."

"Week-old clam chowder in a skin suit—"

"Okay, okay, got the picture," Andy interrupts.

"Kim hit him once too," Destiny volunteers, as I eye-check her to maybe stop with the oversharing. She ignores me. "*Aaannd* she had sex with his sister last year."

"Andy doesn't care about any of that," I say loudly, trying to shut the Destiny chatter train down.

"The human hair gel's sister is a lesbian?" Andy asks, suddenly feeling well enough to sit up in the backseat.

Destiny starts giggling, smiles her mega-wattage, I'm-too-fine-to-be-told-what-to-do smile, and launches into my entire three-year, sordid Changer history with Audrey, starting with the Drew year, as besties in love; to Oryon and the ill-fated sex-capade that landed me in an Abider prison cell ("Silver lining: that's where we met!" Destiny footnotes); to Kim, the queer theater groupie who "is full-stop Audrey's family's worst nightmare! Fat, femme, and Asian!"

Destiny begins singing the Kim Chi song—"*Every generation, Beyoncé, Madonna, got nothing on this triple threat, do the fat, femme, and Asian*"—dissolving into hysterical laughter. But I notice Andy is quiet, hanging on every word, trying to follow my multiple-lives story with his Changer-traumatized Static brain.

"So who were you first?" he asks.

"Drew," Destiny answers for me.

"No. I mean before."

"Destiny, pull the car over," I say.

"The hell, Kim?"

"Do it."

And so, parked on the narrow shoulder of I-75, cars whizzing past, the drone of the freeway ringing in our ears, I tell Andy who I was "first." Which is to say, right there in front of Destiny and not a small number of drivers speeding off to wherever drivers speed off to, I tell him I am his long-lost friend Ethan, the guy who trick-or-treated with him in matching Batman costumes, the guy who learned to ollie at his side, the guy who used to have farting contests with him on his parents' leather couch, the guy he trusted to always be there for him, to have his back, the brother from another mother who abruptly moved away before freshman year and ghosted him entirely shortly after that.

When it seems like he doesn't believe me, I say again clearly that I was Ethan, and that I never meant to hurt him, that there are rules, and I followed them back then, but I am done following them, and I hope he can understand, and even if he can't, I hope he can forgive.

Andy says nothing the whole time I'm rambling on. He avoids my gaze, while Destiny vapes out the window, pretending she isn't listening.

Andy gives me nothing but deafening silence after I trail off, me whipping out the old "You wouldn't understand" chestnut, which is the last thing anyone wants to hear, *ever*.

After another full minute or two (which doesn't sound like long, but trust me, it's excruciatingly long when you are marinating in a pool of confessional flop sweat on the side of a busy interstate): "I came to Tennessee trying to find you," Andy admits quietly. "Well, Ethan."

"I know," I say.

Andy chews on his puffy lip. Shrugs. "Mission accomplished, I guess."

"Yay?" I crack sarcastically, fully aware Kim is nothing like the person Andy was searching for. "Ethan is still here."

"Yeah, where?" Andy shoots back, even more wrecked than when we first picked him up.

"Can we get going?" Destiny breaks in. "I'm getting high on gasoline fumes and not in a good way."

I nod. Then Andy and I ride in silence until we reach RaCha's HQ. Before Destiny cuts the engine, I try to turn around and tell Andy I'm sorry again, but he heaves himself from the car and heads up the sidewalk to the warehouse without a word or even a glance behind.

"Farting contests?" Destiny says, lifting an eyebrow. "Bet you won every time."

"You want to have one right now?" I ask, watching Andy through the windshield.

"Girl, you know I don't fart in this V. I'm pure perfection."

"You're pure something."

"What are you going to do about him?" she asks, serious.

"I don't know," I say, and I don't.

"He'll come around. Maybe."

"And if he doesn't?"

"You'll be someone else in a few months," she reminds me.

And there it was—how had I forgotten? All this coming-clean, coming-out, see-me-love-me stuff wasn't going to mean anything if I didn't do it all over again when I changed into my final V.

My final V.

This was all going to end soon. And I would at last have the power to choose who I want to be forever. The realization was both thrilling and paralyzing. It felt a bit like that game people play: *If you could only eat one meal the rest of your life, what would it be?* There's no right answer. Even the best meal of your life gets old after eating it a couple dozen times. You think you want pizza, then you eat pizza ten times in a row, and pizza officially becomes a form of torture.

What if I transform into someone horrible? What if my last year is the worst of all, and I don't want Audrey to know who I am? What if the Council feels the need to school me next year for my sins, and assigns me a "challenging" V? What if? What if? What if?

"Hey! Anxiety junkie, you're home," Destiny says, giving me a light flick on the ear.

"Sorry, I . . ." *Spaced out.*

Destiny puts the car in park, leans in, hugs me tight. "It's all going to be okay," she whispers, holding up her bruised fist for me to bump. "Damn, I punched a neo-Nazi. I'm the black Indiana Jones!" Then: "To Nazi punching."

"To Nazi punching," I answer back, tapping her knuckles to mine.

"Ouch," she winces.

"I love you, Destiny."

"I love you too, loser. Now get your stank butt out of my damn car."

KIM

CHANGE 3-DAY 203

"**W**hat the Charles Dickens were you thinking?" Touchstone Tracy, cooking up a bitter broth of panic and judgment, per her usual. "Protesting? Outing yourself? Outing *US?* Have you lost your mind?"

Tracy is pacing my room, paying me a home visit, courtesy of Turner the Lives Coach, who the minute he got wind of the RaChas action, dispatched every local Touchstone to dress down their designated Changer, before a dozen mini rebellions could ignite from a single protest, even if the initial action so far had little measurable consequence beyond the viral video of Destiny coldcocking Jason.

"Have you even thought about what this could mean for our kind?" Tracy whisper-talks, like we're exchanging spy secrets in a dark parking garage.

"Yes. That's why I did it," I say. "Hiding in the shadows is bullshit."

"You sound like that no-good Benedict *Arnold*," she spits.

"It's fine if *you* like being closeted, but I don't."

"We're not hiding. We're making calculated choices," she says sharply, prompting Snoopy to jump off my bed.

"For whom?" I ask snottily.

"For everyone. For *mankind*. Mercy, Kim. Have you lost

the plot entirely? I thought you'd grown more than this."

I silently watch Snoopy nose the door ajar and slink out, not enjoying the tense energy swirling in the room between me and Tracy.

She presses on as if reading from an official statement: "Our very reason for being is to spread empathy and tolerance, to better ourselves so we can be examples, find Static partners, and make more Changers, so eventually there will be no one left to fear. Changers bleed all souls together, while preserving and honoring all of our differences. We are here to eliminate the concept of otherness."

"Love and light, right?" I snap sarcastically.

"Don't belittle the mission. You're smarter than that."

"Trace? Do you really believe the only way to make change is by flying under the radar? Going along to get along? Tricking people into discovering their better natures? I don't know if you've looked around lately, but the world isn't exactly brimming with better natures. Abiders are on the rise, becoming more violent, more brazen than ever. They're networking, metastasizing."

"Kim, when power is threatened, those in power act out. For our safety, we need to stick to the plan. Stay together. In the many we are one."

"The master's tools will never dismantle the master's house."

At that Tracy's eyes snap shut like she's going to her happy place, a.k.a. a world without me in it. "Oh, for Christmas sake," she says after a beat, eyes jerking back open.

I feel bad for her. In coming here she was trying to do her job, execute orders she believed were right. Tracy is a good soldier, for sure, but she is also a good person. And I am once again making her life a unique hell.

"I know you want the best for me," I start, but she cuts me off.

"For three long years I have done everything I can do for you. Tried to show you the value of others, of your purpose. *Our* shared purpose. And you have chosen your own needs at every turn—"

"Wait a second, that's not fair."

"I never thought I'd say this, but Chase was right about you."

"Keep his name out of your mouth!" I scream, surprised by the break in my voice.

"You don't give a single hoot about anything but your own desires in the moment," she continues.

"Enough."

"You're right, Kim. Enough. I've failed. You want to tell the world about us, put everyone and everything we stand for at risk, that's on you. But I won't be a part of it."

And with that, Tracy marched out, chin forward, back rod-straight. I could practically smell her indignation as she passed by me.

I should be more invested, but in what's becoming something of a theme in my life—I'm kind of not. I didn't ask for any of this. Why is it my job to teach idiots that they should care about other people? News flash: dolts like Jason will never, ever care about freaks like me. Certain people will always hate "the gays" and "the blacks" and "the Jews" and "the Muslims" and "the foreigners" and "the feminists" and "the poor" and "the differently abled" and any other group that seems to pose a threat to their fragile house of dominance cards. Jason and his Abider-leaning goons are not going to wake up one day and realize they've been stunted zealots their whole lives and start driving for Meals on Wheels or working shifts on the LGBTQ suicide hotline.

If my year as Kim has shown me anything, it's that the appetite for cruelty among certain people is never sated. Queen beyotch Chloe could never get past the way I appear. My size alone was enough for her to assign me to a box and duct-tape the lid shut. Okay, sure, being Kim helped *me*. I grew. (Ha ha, did I.) But so what? Was I such a jerk before? According to Tracy, I'm a bigger jerk today. So maybe, hear me out, this whole Changer thing is an epic, outdated fail, especially in these times. And if it *is*, then why in the hell would I stick with the program?

I don't care if the Council is monitoring these Chronicles. I'm going rogue. Full stop. And the best part of that is that I am going to meet up with Audrey, and I am going to walk her through the whole twisted shebang, and I know—I *know*—she is going to finally see how she is my person.

What else could possibly happen?

KIM

CHANGE 3-DAY 205

I heard about the fire from Andy first. He showed up at the door of my house, duffel bag in hand, trying to act like he was still pissed at me, but so obviously scared and lost he couldn't hold his bitch face.

"It's gone," he said.

"What?"

"The whole place, RaChas HQ. Torched to ash. Apocalypse-level stuff."

"What? How?"

"Abiders, probably. Maybe they were tipped off after the coming-out march," he said.

"Jesus. Was anybody hurt?" I asked, flashing on Benedict and some of my other RaChas roommates from when I lived at HQ during my depression.

"No. Benedict had pretty much cleared everybody out while he was 'reestablishing healthy boundaries' and 'reinstituting his self-care regime.'"

Of course he was.

"Most of the RaChas were squatting with friends or in shelters, except me and Zeke and Layla. Layla was actually sleeping when the fire started, and she tried to grab some equipment, but as it was, she barely got out of there herself."

"What were you doing?"

"I was helping Benedict load up his car for what he called his 'journey to me' road trip."

"Sounds like a book my mother would recommend to her single-mom clients," I said.

"We'd gone to get the tires pumped when we heard the sirens. By the time we made it back, the whole building was in flames."

I didn't know what to say. "Come in. We'll figure something out."

I had no idea what I was going to say to my parents. Bringing in a Static from your pre-Changer past was well outside of protocol. I knew my dad would crap a Changer brick, especially with his ever-increasing role at Changers Central. But this was Andy. My first friend.

I figured I could count on Mom to see past the rules to the person. Andy was a refugee who needed harboring. He had no place left to go. And he figured out the Changers thing all by himself, more or less. Benedict leaked the deets. Not me. I would NEVER break Changer Rule Number One.

At least that's how I spun it to Mom, after I swear I saw sparks shoot from her brain through her ears when Andy walked in and dropped his bag on the carpet.

She kept it together as well as she could, rushing over and smothering him in a full mom-style hug, peppering him with a million questions about where he's been, how he found us, when his voice grew so deep, and of course if he wanted a chicken-and-chili-cheese burrito.

Andy seemed grateful, if a bit embarrassed. After a few minutes he excused himself to go to the bathroom, and that's when Mom turned to me and made the gritted-teeth emoticon face.

"Your father is going to freak," she says flatly, soon as Andy's out of earshot.

"I'm sorry, I didn't know what else to do," I reply. "His dad kicked him out."

"I'll handle Dad," she whispers.

I practically leap into her arms. "Thanks, Mom. I swear I didn't plan on this—he showed up unannounced at RaChas HQ."

"We can talk about all that later. But bottom line is, we can't turn him out on the streets. I suspect your father and I will want to tell his parents he's alive."

"I'm not sure they care," I say.

"Of course they do."

I drop the argument, for now. The important thing is Andy has a temporary home. And I have a chance to make it right with him again.

"I can't believe they burned down HQ. What if you were still living there?" Mom asks then, shoulders giving a small shiver.

"There are some really messed-up people in this world, Mom. People who want us dead and gone. People who'd rather us burn alive than open their hearts to something different."

"I know that, sweet pea. History is rife with cruelty."

It seems like she could cry. I sense a part of her is as skeptical as I am of the Changer mission's ability to right the wrongs of the past. If anyone understands the limits of human growth, it's a shrink.

"Change never comes as fast as we want it to," she acknowledges. "But the arc of progress bends toward the light."

"Okay, Turner Lives Coach."

"I'm serious," she persists, ignoring my sass. "And the brighter that light gets, the harder the dark forces try to extinguish it. In some ways, the rise of the Abiders, the escalation of their violence, proves that Changers are winning the war. The Abiders are scared. They feel their obsolescence coming like a hard, cleansing rain."

"You sound like an end-times movie preview," I joke, assuming the deep baritone of the omnipresent film-trailer narrator: "In a world filled with pain and hate, an unlikely hero emerges . . ."

". . . A hero like none other, one the forces of evil did not see coming," Mom chimes in, in the same cheesy deep voice.

"A girl! Of size! Who likes other girls! Can you believe that shit?" I intone, doing the last bit in my best Aziz Ansari voice.

We both fall out laughing. Mom kisses me on the cheek, tells me in the movie voice that I should check on Andy "before it's too late."

Sitting on my bed, I think about what she said. I want to trust that the world is moving toward tolerance and a widening circle of what it means to be a human in all its myriad forms and permutations. I want to know that kids like me, and Kris, and Michelle Hu, and even Audrey for that matter, will not have to grow up afraid of having to live in some oppressive *Handmaid's Tale* nightmare, but from what I can see, from what I have lived in all my lives so far, that sounds like the stuff of fantasy. The Jasons of the world don't seem

scared to me. They don't suffer. They don't have to look over
their shoulder when they walk down the street. They seem
more brazen and confident in their beliefs than ever.

Andy knocks at the door, interrupting my doom spiral.
"Cool if I come in?"

"Duh, dummy."

He enters slowly, eyes darting around like he's searching
for something specific. Evidence of Ethan, I guess.

"Nice space," he says.

"Thanks," I say.

"This is as awkward as a plane fart." He grimaces.

"Yeah. But it doesn't have to suck." I'm trying to see Kim
through his POV. Wondering what he thinks of her. What
he *would* think of her if he didn't know it was me.

"It doesn't?" he asks.

"Would you rather I was Destiny?" I give him a seduc-
tive shimmy.

"Oh, man. Don't do that."

"Don't you think I'm sexxxy? *I'm too sexy for my cat, too
sexy for my blouse, too sexy for my car,*" I start singing.

"Dude, those are not the words."

"*Too sexy for my sandwich, too sexy for my jeans—*"

"I'm begging you to stop!" Andy lets out a goofy moan
of despair. It feels a little like old times, me and Andy acting
like idiots.

I stand up, dance the robot. "*I'm too sexy for my external
hard drive, for my animatronic limbs.*"

Andy hops up, starts dancing too, both of us executing
the lamest pop-and-lock-routine on record.

"*Too sexy for my empty, cavernous soul, too sexy for Sylvia*

Plath, too sexy for Kid Rock, I mean Robert Ritchie," I sing, Andy laughing louder and harder until we both tire out, collapsing, breathing heavy, side by side on my bed.

I turn my head, stare right into his eyes, get a thought but hold it in—because Andy will think it's weird. But then I can't help it and it just blurts out: "I've kind of missed you. It's been hard, doing this on my own, when nobody knows me like you do."

Andy jerks his chin toward the ceiling, breaking my gaze, but I press on: "I get that this is bonkers, that it feels like a sick joke. But I didn't ask for it. And I never wanted to leave you behind. I needed you."

"Sure you did," Andy chokes out, swiveling his head even farther away from mine.

"I did. I always did. Because Ethan doesn't exist without you."

Andy sits up, heads toward the door like he's leaving, then freezes. "Well, the Ethan I knew," he starts stiffly, still facing away, as I feel my skin prick with tension, "was a terrible, terrible . . . singer."

"Suck it," I say.

"And an even worse dancer. So it seems to me like he is more or less still in the picture."

In an instant, I feel years of shame dissolve. I try and keep it together so as not to spoil the moment. "Like you're Travis freaking Wall."

"Who the hell is Travis Wall?" he asks. "Is that a chick thing?"

"Piss off. And, totally."

"You want a Coke, spazmatron?" he asks.

"I'm too sexy for a Coke, too sexy for a clichéd version of sexxxxxy," I shoot back, as Andy spins around and moonwalks down the hall toward the kitchen.

The rest of the night we didn't talk about anything but graphic novel Harley Quinn versus movie Harley Quinn, and whether men's soccer is better than women's soccer (it isn't), and how we'd both 1,000 percent have sex with Jennifer Lopez even though she's older than our moms. Then we watched serial killer documentaries on Netflix, ate nachos and cinnamon toast, and used Twizzlers as straws in our Cokes.

We said nothing about anything that mattered. (Something that mattered more to me than I can say.)

KIM

CHANGE 3-DAY 207

"**E**than didn't care about outfits, dude," Andy says from my bed, where he's playing vintage *GTA* like we used to.

"No, seriously, which one?" I ask, holding up two shirts in front of my chest.

"The one on the left," he mumbles.

"You're not even looking!" I whine, throwing the white Ramones T-shirt on the floor and opting to go with a plain black one.

"Do you think Destiny would go out with me?" Andy asks for the 147th time since meeting her.

"She's with DJ," I remind him for the 147th time.

"So?"

"Have you seen DJ? The two of them are so blindingly perfect together it's like they were made in a lab. They're like those photos that come in the *Just Married* frames when you buy them from Target."

"Gross."

"But #truth," I note.

I step into the bathroom and close the door behind me, peel off my stale top, throw on the clean black one. I check myself in the mirror, wet my hair and massage some putty into it, slicking back the long part on top. I look like an Asian Lea DeLaria. Not the worst. I slap on some pale-pink

lip gloss, a swipe of electric-blue eye[s] [at?]
the corners, cat's-eye style. When J[   ]
room, Andy glances up.

"Hey there, David Bowie."

"Ha." I pop my tee at the wa[ist]

"You seem nervous," Andy says, press[ing] [a]
game.

"That obvious?"

"Kinda."

"Does this shirt make it seem like I've given up?" I ask.

"On what?"

"I look like a roadie for a cover band, right?"

"No."

"Is it too boxy?"

"What even is that? Like a boxer? Or . . . ?"

"What if she doesn't believe me?" I blurt, simultaneously realizing that 1) Andy's probably the worst person to ask, but 2) nobody else is aware that I'm spilling everything to Audrey tonight, so he's kind of the only game in town.

"She might not," Andy says, pulling no punches and clearly still smarting from the sting of the Changer-related dramas in his own life, one of them right in front of him, asking him for advice. "It's pretty messed up, like *Twilight Zone* shit. You're basically a comic book mutant, minus the lab accident."

"Gee, thanks," I say, scanning the room for my wallet.

"You need to give her a break. As hard as this is for you, it's going to blow her mind. You may want to wear a Hannibal plastic kill-suit to protect yourself from splattering brain matter."

do you know about brain matter?"

y flips me the bird. "Listen, if you love this girl, you
o allow her whatever she needs to get her head around
situation. I don't think you have any idea how it feels
when a person you love vanishes from your life."

"That's where you're wrong," I say peevishly, memories
of Chase flooding in, memories of my past lives and the
people who knew me, and how all of that got sandblasted
into oblivion every year. "My whole teenage life is about being ghosted. I mean, if you want to get technical about it, I
AM a fucking ghost."

"Whatever." Andy's not buying it.

"Do you think she's going to hate me?"

"No idea."

"Andy, please."

He sighs. "Well, I don't."

It's then I notice the bracelet on my desk. I instinctively
grab it, a concrete talisman that Audrey can touch and hold
whenever what I'm trying to explain to her seems like a drug
trip gone extra wrong.

"What's the worst that can happen?" Andy asks.

"Wellll, the Changers Council can forcibly extricate me
from my home and throw me in a compulsory compliance-
training program for the rest of my Cycle—OH, HEY,
DAD!"

"What about compliance training?" my dad asks, popping his head into my room.

"Excuse me?" I bluff.

Andy smiles and waves, "Good afternoon, Mr. Miller."

Dad steps in, glances back and forth between Andy and

me, clearly suspicious, then relents. "I'm making a run to Costco for the Council's regional party, you guys come and help me load, okay?"

"Sure thing," Andy says.

"I've actually got plans," I say sheepishly.

"Like?"

"Tracy stuff," I lie.

Dad seems onto me—if not specifically, then generally—but also like he's not going to get into it in front of Andy, whom he would prefer weren't even here since it is Bad! Changer! Policy! But Mom worked her psychiatry-guilt mojo on him, making it seem if we turned Andy out he'd become a sad runaway statistic Dad would have to live with for the rest of his Changer days (plus might spill about Changers in a more public way), which was not high on Dad's to-do list.

"Leaving in five," he says, yanking the door shut behind him.

"He's going to grill you in the car," I whisper.

"I got you," Andy says, flashing a cheesy thumbs-up. "Now go get that girl."

Audrey is outwardly skittish, her voice warbling when she suggests we go for a walk by the water instead of sitting at Starbucks to talk about the incredibly intimate, uh, stuff that's happened between us.

The Cumberland River is low and dark, the air still, only a handful of mosquitoes buzzing around our faces and nipping the fleshy inside of our elbows.

"It's nice here," Audrey says as we tentatively make our

way down the bank of the river on the well-worn path, side-stepping roots and slick patches of red clay. "I don't come here often enough."

"Oh snap, that was my next line: *Do you come here often?*"

Audrey gives a weak smile.

"So," I say after a few more steps.

"So."

"Soooo," I say again. "I suppose I should start at the beginning."

"*A very fine place to start,*" Audrey sings, then stops, her gaze casting down at the bracelet on my arm. "I'll never get used to seeing that on your wrist."

She reaches into her back pocket, pulls out a folded-up piece of paper, starts opening it, the creases weathered and soft from folding and unfolding. Before the paper is flattened all the way, I know what it is: the e-mail I sent. The vomiting-up of Changer chunks I wrote that night I was stoned. Uncensored gibberish I never intended to send, but Benedict sent on my behalf, without my knowledge, because Benedict lives in a Victorian comedy of errors where high jinks and heartbreak only mean everything works out in the end.

"I was high when I wrote that!" I exclaim.

"So you've said. But is it true?" Audrey asks.

I try to remember exactly what I typed out. "Essentially. I think. Probably."

"I thought it was some sort of sick prank," she says. "Cruel and mean."

"I didn't send it, a friend did. You can tell—I mean, it's obvious how it wasn't finished at the end, right? I mean, you were never meant to see . . ." I start blathering, but it doesn't matter. It feels like I'm caught in a lie about a lie about a lie about a lie.

Audrey gestures toward a bench facing the river. We walk over, take a seat, sit hip to hip. She hands me the note. "I don't want to decipher this anymore. I don't want to be in the dark, feeling stupid and lost. Tell me what this is all about."

I take the paper from her hand, breathing in so deep it shocks my lungs. I glance over the letter while I try to think about what I'm going to say to her right now.

Dear Audrey,

I know this is going to sound crazy. Wow, how long have I wanted to say that to you? Anyway, so, this is Kim. Kim Cruz, from school. I hope you got home okay last night. That dance kind of went off the rails, huh?

Anyway, I don't know how else to say this, but, it felt like we had a connection last night. Like we've known each other for lifetimes. (Do you believe in that stuff?) I've never felt that about anybody before, which I figure is really rare, so why not just nut up and tell you?

The thing is, we kind of have known each other for lifetimes. Maybe not lifetimes. Well, for me they are.

If you're still reading this, which I would under-stand if you're not, but bear with me, because here's the thing: I've been at Central longer than just this year. In fact, I have been in your life over the last two and a half years. I've seen you through a lot of ups and downs, a close friendship with a girl who moved away, and then

43

a relationship with a guy who also left school, suddenly, last spring. I know all about Romeo & Juliet. (Boy do I.) Cheerleading. Your brother. Your mother's cooking.

For two years I feel sort of like I've been your invisible protector. (From this guy named Kyle, which is a whole other story.) Anyway, I've loved you every step of the way.

I know you didn't ask for this. It's just, there are things in the universe we can't explain. Actual magic that brings people into each other's lives for a reason. Like I've been brought into yours.

Again, I understand if you want nothing to do with me after reading this. It is admittedly cuckoo for Cocoa Puffs. But what do I have to lose at this point? I can't help but feel that you felt this THING last night between us. You sensed that history too.

So if you did, can you let me know? Maybe we could spend some time together. Trust me, it wouldn't be the strangest thing that ever happened.

&(^^%%!%$#*(&**&#$^\$%#&)*)*(&)*^&^>?? ?!?!?!!!!?

What am I doing why am I writing this I must be freaking insane in the membrane. She is going to think I'm bonkers and never want to talk to me again don't press send don't press send don't press senddddddd.

"Well, this is a real shit sandwich," I acknowledge, stating the obvious. The fun, freeing part of outing myself to Audrey ending; the terrifying, messed-up one about to begin. "I'm really sorry about all this."

"But what exactly is *this*?" she demands, loud enough that a couple of runners look our way as they pass behind us on the path. "I feel like I'm in a live version of *The Manchurian Candidate*."

I take a controlled breath. *Me too, girl.* "Forget the mind-splintering oddity for a minute. The most important thing, the thing that's never *not* been true, is that I've loved you since the minute I spotted you in homeroom freshman year."

"When you were Drew?"

"I'll never forget that morning, when you made me feel like a human again after Chloe fashion-shamed my hair and clothes. And then when class ended, you pointed me toward the girls' bathroom, when I was about to go into the boys'."

"Yeah. What was that about?" Audrey asks, her eyebrows knit tightly like she's solving a riddle.

I decide to come out with it: "Before I was Drew, I was a guy named Ethan."

"Wait, what? Meaning, you transitioned?" Audrey leans back on the bench, her head swiveling back and forth, bewildered and unable to do the math, which, who could, really? "More than once?"

"Yes and no." I sigh. "Bear with me. This gets real convoluted, real quick."

"You could say that."

I watch Audrey's face as she turns toward the river, my skin growing hot, self-loathing lighting me up from inside.

"So Oryon?" she prods.

"I'm Oryon."

"I thought you were Drew."

"I'm Drew too. Also."

Audrey exhales, steals another glance at the bracelet she gave Drew on the last day of freshman year. "Tell me something only Drew would know."

"Uh, okay," I begin, not certain where this might end up. "Well, okay. Our kiss at the school dance—"

"As I recall, Drew—uh, *you*—weren't so into that," Audrey says, blushing.

"Are you kidding?"

"I guess it was a pretty public first kiss," she adds.

"Yes, yes, it was," I agree, laughing. "Our big rom-com finale." *Was she flirting with me a little? Focus, Kim.* "Well, actually, here's something nobody but you and I would know. We were ABOUT to kiss two times before that. In Mr. Crowell's class when we performed that scene from *Romeo and Juliet*, and then in your bedroom that night I slept over, when you wanted to practice—"

"But Jason burst in on us," she interrupts. "Acting like Cujo on two legs. And you, I mean Drew, stood up to him. Kim, I mean *you*, do that too." Audrey shyly drops her chin toward her feet.

"You can just say *you*. Don't worry about all the versions. They're all me."

"God, I feel like my brain is made of cottage cheese."

"Did you have a crush on me then? As Drew?" I ask, not completely sure I want the answer.

"Don't be an idiot," she says, blushing.

Man, I really want to kiss her.

But I don't.

We fall into an uncomfortable silence. I catch myself

thinking of the night we slept together, how she seemed so into Oryon, so trusting and calm in my arms. I swallow a million questions I am dying to ask. Like, who did she care for most? Who was she most attracted to? Which version of me captured her heart? These are selfish questions, and I know it. This isn't about her making me feel better. It's about me making her feel less insane. And more safe.

A boat motors by with a large caramel-colored poodle on the bow, barking into the wind. Audrey suggests we resume walking then, but before we get up, I turn and put a hand on her shoulder, and ask her to swear never to tell anybody about the information I'm giving her. That there are potential life-and-death consequences, that people have been killed as a result of what I'm sharing, and it isn't pretty, and it hurts, and it could change things irrevocably, and so it is to be taken seriously.

"You're scaring me," she whispers.

"I trust you," I say. Then I open the floodgates. About the new V each year of high school. About my Touchstone Tracy, and how every Changer gets a mentor like that, someone who is also a Changer. How the Council arranges everything logistically with schools and housing. Rules about parents coming to campus, the feints we are given to explain where kids disappear to after each year of school. I can see her eyes widen with each revelation.

"And at the end of the Cycle, we pick one of our four V's to live as forever; there's even a special ceremony right after graduation," I finish.

"So you're going to be a whole new person next year?"

I nod my head slowly.

"Who?"

"No freaking idea," I admit, and I can tell she doesn't necessarily love that part either.

"Can you go back to Ethan?"

"No."

"Wow. Never?"

"Never," I say.

"Why not?"

"We can never go back to who we were before the changes."

Audrey falls silent for a few moments. Then says, "That must be so terrible for your mom."

If there was ever a Static who doesn't need empathy lessons, it's Audrey.

"I think she's o-okay," I stammer. "For the most part. How about you? Are you okay?"

She nods, half-smiles. "For the most part."

Encouraged, I continue, deciding to take Audrey even deeper through the labyrinth of Changers rules. She listens quietly, nodding her head, sometimes cocking it to the left in that cute way she does when things seem particularly confounding.

"Why can't Changers get with other Changers?" she asks.

"Counter to the mission. I guess it's kind of like dating someone in your own family."

"What ever happened to that Chase guy from your Bickersons band?" she asks randomly, like she just remembered him. "The one who beat Jason to a pulp after he tried to . . ."

And like that, a switch flips, and the tears pour down my face. I try, but I can't say anything else, cannot get words out. And if I could, what words would they be? That Chase died so I could live?

Audrey leans in, embraces me for longer than I ever thought would be possible again. "I'm so sorry," she says.

"It's not your fault," I manage, loving the way her arms feel around me.

We fall silent again.

"Can I ask if your mom or dad is the Changer?" Audrey eventually asks.

"My dad."

"How did your mom find out?"

"I don't really know," I realize, hardly believing I've never asked them the details of their courtship, or the big reveal of when Dad told Mom he was a Changer, what she said, how she reacted. Maybe if I had, I would be doing this better. Though Audrey seems to be handling it well enough.

The setting sun throws a veil of pink across the river's glassy surface as Audrey and I finally start walking back. I sense something in her has softened. After a few steps, I take her hand in mine. At first she flinches, but she doesn't pull away entirely. So I squeeze a little harder, and she lets me thread my fingers between hers.

We walk like that in silence until we get to the bridge. And it is there that I decide there's one last disclosure I need to make. I have to tell her about Oryon. What happened to him that night. Why I abandoned her. Only, I need to do it in a way that leaves her brother out of it. I can't be the one who makes him potentially complicit in my kidnapping or in Chase's beating and the death that came from it, especially since the Council has no hard evidence that Jason was even in the gang that jumped me. Not yet, anyway.

Jason is a monster in a thousand ways, but if I'm going to have any chance of keeping Audrey on team Changer/ Kim, I can't force her to choose between her family and me. Above all, I need to make it clear Oryon's abduction had nothing to do with her, or anything she did. Because Audrey would never forgive herself.

"But why?" Audrey asks for maybe the tenth time. "Why did they want to hurt *you*?"

"It wasn't me, specifically. There's this group of people out there who suspect they know about Changers and are scared of us, I guess," I try to explain.

Audrey seems like she's deep in thought, about her church maybe. Or her brother.

"It was terrible timing. After what we shared that night—I swear, the best night of my life, all my lives, hands down." (Audrey smiles a little at that.) "And then the bracelet. I was going to tell you everything when I saw you, but I never got a chance because they picked me up the next day when I was out walking Snoopy."

"But how did they find you?" she persists, something niggling at her, even if she isn't putting two and two together yet.

"No idea," I say, shutting her inquiry down. "So anyway, I was withdrawn from school, recovering at Changers Central through the end of the year, no phone, no Internet, explicit restrictions on all non-Changers communications so as to make sure those Abiders weren't able to find me or any of the others again."

"It's so horrible," Audrey says. "I can't imagine what it was like in that basement, not sure you'd survive."

"It wasn't so bad," I sigh. But it kind of was.

"If only I hadn't run out of the apartment like a crazy person," Audrey says, anger and guilt in her voice now, "and called my brother to give me a ride home. Maybe we would have been walking your dog together that morning, or . . ."

"Look at me." I gently take Audrey's chin in my hand. "You are the bravest, kindest, most accepting person I know. Thank you for letting me share all of this with you. Anybody else would have melted down and bailed."

"But I'm the reason you got abducted."

"I got abducted because of who I am, and what people in this world fear about who I am. That has *nothing* to do with you." And then, because she seems so inconsolably sad, I add one last thing: "No matter what happens from here on out, I'll never keep anything from you again."

"You swear?" she responds, apparently relieved for the moment. "You'll tell me the truth, always?"

"I swear," I say. And I mean it.

KIM

CHANGE 3-DAY 265

You know that nineties song "Dreams Can Come True"? If you don't, you can listen to the inside of my head right now because that jam is on an endless loop:

Just a question of time I knew we'd be together
And that you'd be mine, I want you here forever
Do you hear what I'm saying gotta say how I feel
I can't believe you're here but I know that you're real . . .

Dreams can come true
Look at me babe I'm with you . . .

I'm officially proclaiming it the "Audrey and me" theme song, because not only does it sum up the past three years of our roller-coaster romance, but it also lays down the unicorn wonder starburst moment that is happening this instant. Because, yeah baby, like the proverbial band, Audrey and I are back together.

After all my pining and depression and living in a self-dug hole of misery for, oh, a whole freaking year, Audrey has come around, and by *come around* I mean we had sex.

Boom.

It happened yesterday when I picked her up on my Vespa

and we drove downtown, hanging out on a blanket by what I now think of as OUR river, watching the old-fashioned tourist paddleboats putter by, listening to playlists she'd made—heavy with songs from the Cure and Tegan and Sara, I might add. She confided she'd made some of the lists weeks ago with me in the back of her mind.

She'd never really been able to shake me, even though she didn't know why. That fluke night at the bowling alley when I impressed her with my give-no-effs at karaoke had something to do with it. How much fun she had, despite herself. And now that she did know, meaning KNOW the truth of who I am, all the chips fell into place, and the more time we spent together our last couple months, the easier it became for her to spot Drew and Oryon in me, to see all of *me* in general, and well, as the sun began to set, and we moved our blanket behind some trees, one song led to a peck on the head, which led to a kiss, which led to a grope, which led to Audrey suddenly climbing on top of me, pulling the second blanket over us and letting herself go wild in a way I'd never seen before.

It was, all told, a glorious night.

Even if the ride home was a little strange. Lucky the wind was loud, and we couldn't hear much through our helmets. I think Audrey was embarrassed. It's like she surprised herself. Maybe she had some regret. But I didn't care. I mean, I care about her, which would be obvious to a blind-ass bat from space. But I didn't care to plumb whatever fears or second thoughts Audrey was wrestling with in her busy brain because I'd just had sex with the woman I love for the second time, and that was a high I was going to ride for as long as possible.

Bee-Tee-Dubs, I'm still on that high.

It's not just the sex. (Okay, it's a lot about the sex.) Some of my unbridled joy is the unique satisfaction that comes from being right about a person. Audrey is the Audrey I've always suspected her to be. Deep and soulful and above trivial concerns like physical appearance. Though I confess I was freaking when she reached under my shirt, her hands settling on my chest with such gentleness and acceptance, I swear my soul flew from my body.

Audrey found a way to love me as Kim. Not that Kim is unlovable. But Kim is no Oryon. She's not a Drew. She's not typical or traditional or conventional or the image anyone sees celebrated in any media ever. Chubby Asian girls aren't exactly popping up on all the lit feeds. Kim, in modern America, for all its claim to diversity and acceptance, is invisible. But as it turns out, none of that mattered, because Audrey connected with my insides.

(Boy did she.)

(Sorry.)

(Not sorry.)

Audrey confessed she'd realized she'd let herself get caught up in trying to be "normal" this year in school, because she was sick of fighting so hard to be different in her family, at school, with queen bee Chloe. Different wasn't all it was cracked up to be. No matter how much they try and sell it in the soda ads.

"Preaching to the choir," I said, and she kissed me on the mouth hard, like an apology.

Later, when I Facetimed Kris and told him that Audrey and

I slept together, and that SHE initiated it, he of course insisted on hearing every sordid detail, squealing with delight whenever a nipple entered the picture.

"So now I have two mommies?" he joked.

"That might be premature. I'm not sure she's ready to be a card-carrying LGBTQ-club kid."

"Um, from what you've just shared, she could be president of the club."

Kris was still living with his drag mother, channeling every queen he met, wandering through the wilderness of his sexual and gender identity, assuming he was THE expert in the subject, blissfully naïve to the truth that his best buddy Kim was part of a race of people obliterating the very conceits of gender and sexuality to begin with.

"Vice president," I say, and Kris laughs.

"Treasurer, because girlfriend was all about your coin purse," he cracks.

"Gross."

"Shanté, you stay," he declares in his best RuPaul voice.

"You sashay away."

"Mopping is stealing."

"You really need to stop watching *Paris Is Burning* on Netflix every day," I say.

"And you really need to stop being a boring-ass drag, you big lez."

"Who are you calling *big*?" I joke.

I watch Kris smiling on the tiny screen in his vintage perforated tank top and high-waisted jeans, and it hits me that in a few weeks, unless I decide to put him in the circle of trust, we won't be friends anymore.

Because I won't be Kim anymore.

"So when's your next sex bout?" he asks.

"I'm having it now."

Kris does a full-on fake puke. "Did you read that article in *Nat Geo* about how there are gay dolphins? Legit same-sex dolphin couples. Put that in your homosexuality-is-unnatural pipe and smoke it, phobic arseholes." I hear a gravelly voice in the background asking Kris about cigarettes. "I'm happy for you, you stupid bitch," he says, "but I gotta go."

"Me too."

"Now find me a freak to love."

"Shouldn't be a problem. I know a *lot* of freaks." I point at him, and Kris blows me a kiss as the screen freezes, then goes black.

I try Facetiming Audrey after that, but she doesn't pick up. I push down the worry that immediately crowds my thoughts. Worry that she is scouring the dark web for a drug to vanish any trace in her head of our afternoon by the river. Worry that Jason somehow senses a ripple in his Abider-leaning matrix and has cornered Audrey in her bedroom, screaming at her with a megaphone about the dangers of hanging with anyone who doesn't look like one of those kids from *Cabaret* who sing "Tomorrow Belongs to Me." Who am I kidding? That's every night at Audrey's house.

I try Facetiming Destiny. She texts that she can't pick up, says to call like it's 1999 or some crap. So I old-school phone her.

"Hey, girl," she says when she picks up. "How's sweet, sad Andy?"

"Fine. Sweet. Sad. Still in love with you."

"Awwww."

"So. I had sex with Audrey."

"Hello! Why didn't you say so?"

"I just did."

"Man. That's major. Beyond. How do you feel? How *was* it?"

"Remember the rain scene in *The Notebook*?" I say.

"Yeah."

"Like that, only sunny."

"So, not the worst." Destiny laughs.

"No. Not the worst." I laugh back. Then proceed to tell her all the gories. And, of course, my irrational fears.

"Not so irrational, given the history there," Destiny observes.

I knew she was right. Making Audrey my Static is like trying to thread a needle with my feet. An uphill battle, at best. Premature, according to every Changers and Static standard since the final decades of the twentieth century. But you can't choose who you love. Right? Or when you love.

"Don't take this the wrong way," Destiny says, "but my priority is you. Your safety. Your heart. You're a goddamned jewel, and from what I've seen, that family is *Shining*-level scary."

I stay quiet.

Destiny continues: "I mean, her brother? He's like a car alarm that never shuts off. And her parents? I don't know, Kim."

"You're not wrong, but—"

"But." I hear her sigh on the other end of phone. "You're sure this is what you want?"

"Yes."

"Then I'm here for it."

"Thanks, Destiny."

"What are you going to do about the fall? Your last V?" she asks.

"I promised to tell her."

Another long sigh.

"I'm tired of lying," I add.

"I hear you. But . . ."

"But what?"

"You have no idea what's going to happen next year. Can you trust her?"

"Yes," I say defensively.

"Dang, DJ's texting. Gotta go. Be careful."

It's three a.m. I can't sleep. It's like I have a big test tomorrow. I check the clock every hour. In a way, I do have a test. School is ending in less than two weeks. Audrey will go to her hidey-hole church camp. I will be stuck here. Odds are we won't see each other until the first day of my final V. Which could be anything. I could be anyone. Anyone but Kim. Or Oryon. Or Drew. Or Ethan. In the end, Audrey loved all of them in a way. More than I loved them myself.

When people get married, they're supposed to stick together through anything. For better or worse. Sickness and health. Hell or high water. That's what love is supposed to do. But the divorce stats tell a different story. All people change, and the people who love them often hate the change, and then that's that.

It's four a.m. And I'm spiraling. I've always been a spiraler. I guess Ethan's overthinking and struggles with anxiety are one of the lovely bonuses that stuck with me through every change. Couldn't have been his coordination or his thick hair.

I try to do deep breathing. Simply be. Simply be. In the moment.

Why can't I be happy? I started this day so high and confident. Dreams can come true. Blah blah blah. A few hours later, the nightmares are setting in every time I doze off. I would do almost anything to get a handle on my brain, to be able to shut it down. I know how lucky I am. I'm not breaking brick in a Scientology work camp. I have amazing friends and parents who love me, and yet, *spin spin spin*. The what-if thought train barreling down my track.

I guess sex does complicate things.

At least this time I'm not getting postcoitally abducted. Hijacked by my insecurities, maybe.

How early is too early to text Audrey before school?

KIM

CHANGE 3-DAY 267

Parking my scooter in the student lot and bending over to lock the wheel, I hear the familiar rumble: Jason's car screaming into the roundabout in front of school. It screeches to a halt so that everybody notices—the wormhole of insecurity in this dude knows no bottom—and Audrey steps out. She doesn't really acknowledge or say goodbye to him, just slams the door. I wait until he speeds off (more tire-squealing so every Central student within earshot has to check him out), and then I stay close to the side of the building (okay, lurk) while I consider how to approach Audrey.

After following a safe distance behind her for what any outside observer might consider a creepy amount of time, I get the courage to call out a soft and nonthreatening, "Hey," which startles her nonetheless.

"Hey," she echoes.

"What's up? How are you feeling?" I ask, trying not to be too obvious I'm referencing the whole sex thing.

"I'm okay," she says. "You?"

I can't tell which way this is going. She's staring at me with no expression, the student body floating by on the warm breeze, amped up to be headed into their last full week of the school year. It's like she's been shot with a tranquilizer dart.

"Soooo," I say.

"So."

"Yeah, so."

"Soooooo." She exhales sharply, the breath popping her bangs up over her forehead.

"This chemistry is electric," I try, cracking a hint of a smile to hopefully break the awkwardness. It doesn't.

I'm officially freaking out on the inside, but doing everything in my power not to reveal even a flicker of anxiety on the outside. I'm running cool-girl exit lines in my head when all of a sudden Audrey launches toward me. For a split-second I think she's coming in for a hug, but then I realize that Chloe has blown past, shoving Audrey from behind.

"Chubby chase much?" Chloe hisses as she and her crew strut past.

I put a hand out to catch Audrey before she falls, and we burst out laughing, the postsex tension bubble bursting.

"I guess Chloe didn't get the message that fat-shaming is so five years ago," I say, as Audrey rights herself. "Girlfriend is not on trend."

Audrey smiles wanly. "I can't believe how much time I wasted with her."

"I can't either."

"Thanks."

"What did y'all even talk about?" I ask.

"Lot of makeup tutorials. Lot of thirsty posting for Instagram likes."

"Symbiotic."

"You know, I once caught her lifting images from this New York party girl's account and using them on her own."

"No way. That's tragic." (As I'm saying this it occurs to

61

me that hiding within the lives of other people may not be only a Changer imperative.)

"She's a sad little character. I kind of feel bad for her," Audrey says.

"You feel bad for the hateful narcissist who wishes us dead?"

Audrey snorts. "Kinda."

I fight the urge to kiss her on the lips. Behind us, the bell rings.

"We should go," Audrey says, not moving.

"We totally should," I say, not moving either.

When we finally make it to homeroom, Mr. Crowell is still avoiding direct contact with me. Instead, he nervously flits about, fingering his skinny tie, flipping through papers on his cluttered desk, flopping and reflopping his hair. Tracy has told him all about the visibility march and how I was endangering Changer-kind for my own selfish ends, so I'm sure he has no idea what to say to me. (I wonder if Mr. Crowell ever regrets getting involved in this wack alternate universe—or with Tracy for that matter.)

Audrey and I sit next to each other in the back of class— Kris flanking me on the other side, batting his lashes like dragonfly wings.

"Hey there, kitty girl," he greets Audrey, who blushes and waves. Then to me: "Where's the brother?"

"Off campus at physical therapy rehabbing his busted knee."

"Never thought I'd be in favor of police brutality," Kris snarks; I shoot him a look. "Too far?"

At lunch, four of us (Audrey, Kris, Michelle Hu, and I) perch at the end of the nerd table, Michelle droning on about the upcoming Lego League robotics camp. I'd assured Audrey I hadn't told Kris much of anything about the s-e-x, but of course it's obvious Kris knows *everything*, because Kris has a poker face like Lady Gaga, which is to say, he does not have one at all.

I keep imploring him with my eyes to knock off the U-Haul and Electrelane references, but the more I make faces, the more Kris revels in his contraband knowledge. Meanwhile, I'm praying to the Changer gods that Audrey remembers Kris doesn't know about me, that she won't slip and mention the whole changing-into-four-different-people-during-high-school thing.

Watching the two of them converse when each one thinks they know more than the other is a real mind cramp, let me tell you. All the brinkmanship and innuendo flying back and forth makes me want to explode a truth bomb over the entire table like we tried to do at the march. Finally tell all my friends the whole story about me.

But I don't. I guess the points Tracy made have sunk in more than I realized. I want to be out and proud. But outing myself necessarily means outing others who aren't ready, or who could be thrust into danger—and that isn't something I'm so sure I should do anymore.

"Do you have a second?" It's DJ, unexpectedly sidling up at the table.

"Sure," I say, nodding at Audrey and Kris to go ahead and bus their trays without me.

"Hey, DJ," Kris says, lingering.

"Hey, Kris. Dope, uh, blouse."

Kris practically swoons as I nudge him along and away.

"What's wrong?" I ask DJ, who has the air of a guy whose cat has gone missing.

"Is everything okay with Destiny?" he asks.

"Yeah, why?"

He shifts on his feet, lips pinched tight. "Uh, she's, uh," he begins, his voice quieting. "She's not answering any of my calls or texts. I was thinking maybe her phone is broken or . . ."

Crap. Destiny is avoiding DJ in advance of her Forever Ceremony. But I thought he might be her one. Or that she'd at least break it off cleanly, face to face.

"I think she's been having some drama at home," I lie.

"Five seconds ago you said she was fine," he throws back.

"She hasn't been in touch much with me either," I lie again.

"Uh-huh."

This feels gross. Also, not my job. Destiny should be handling her own business. The tortured, confused expression on DJ's face reminds me yet again how morally complicated this whole Changer methodology can be in the Static world. I really like DJ. Hell, we went to jail together last year when we were arrested for not being white. If only I could tell him that. Or that Destiny was once three other teenagers and that her attention is probably elsewhere at this moment because she is mulling over what person she's LITERALLY going to be, though that doesn't mean she doesn't love you, because she really, really does.

"I'll give her a holler tonight and see what's up," I offer.

"Got it," DJ says, composing himself. "I shouldn't have asked. It's not right putting you in the middle."

"Totally not a problem," I say, I putting a hand on his shoulder. "So. I heard you're headed to Yale."

"Yep. Yale drama."

"Is that like regular drama, but smarter? Like, instead of, *Suck a dick, douche bag,* it's all, *You'll henceforth rue the day* and whatnot?"

DJ snorts, not quite allowing himself to laugh. "Something like that."

I try to be helpful: "Listen, maybe Destiny doesn't want to hold you back from of any of these great things headed your way. She probably figures you want to fly and be free."

"She could never be in the way of anything in my life," DJ says, as Audrey approaches and respectfully mouths, *Ready?* because it's time to go to class.

"Everything is going to work out," I lie. Again.

DJ turns, stuffs headphones into his ears, and shuffles off. It's crushing to watch, but selfishly I'm glad I'm never going to have to do to Audrey what Destiny is doing to DJ. Audrey knows everything, and will continue to know everything.

Knowledge is power, and I said as much to Destiny as soon as I got home from school, locking myself in my bedroom to Facetime her and fill her in on DJ's anguish in the cafeteria.

"What else can I do?" she says.

"Do you love him?" I ask.

"Sure . . ."

"Yes or no? Because DJ's a good guy. Like, one of the best."

"Come on," she says, getting a little ticked off, "I'm aware. But do you really think I'm supposed to meet my Static while I'm still in high school? What is this, 1920? Nobody knows what will make them happy forever in high school."

I don't speak.

"Sorry."

"I care about you both," I say, stating the obvious.

"I'm doing this precisely because I care about him," she sighs.

"I know, I know, it's okay."

"It's not okay, Kim!" she snaps. "I didn't go rogue and tell my boyfriend like you told Audrey. Did you ever think that maybe doing that places an unfair burden on her? That maybe rules are there for a reason?"

"I didn't see you worried about rules during the visibility march."

"That was about supporting who we are, showing up for difference. When that video went viral, I told DJ I was marching as an ally to my queer and social activist friends."

"So many lies," I say.

"White lies that protect us and them!"

"But he knows the truth about your feelings for him," I shoot back.

"Yes. And that's nowhere near the same as dumping your whole history on one person and then saying, *Now love me unconditionally even if the next time you see me I look like the Keebler elf, and by the way, you're now required to be complicit in this secret society, or else I might get disappeared.*" Destiny takes a breath. "If I'm not going to be with DJ for the rest of my life, why saddle him with my baggage, with Changer baggage? Until the whole Changer community is out and integrated, it'll only screw him up. The kindness is to maintain the lie."

Watching Destiny lecture me on the small screen on my bed, I feel a jolt deep in my gut. She's kind of right. I never thought about the fact that telling Audrey, especially before I've completed my Cycle of changing, puts her in a pretty messed-up position. What if she's not interested in the person I become next? Even if I'm the "same person on the inside," and she somehow finds a way to let her feelings for Drew and Oryon extend to Kim, it doesn't mean she's necessarily always going to be attracted to my outside. I can hope, but I can't really expect that sort of blind acceptance from her. She shouldn't have to feel all this pressure to be "down" with something that is, let's face it, weird. Never mind that her family is Abider-leaning, at best. Active DL Abiders at worst. Why did I think I could push all that aside? Oh right. Sex.

"Audrey's different," I say. "And I couldn't explain away the bracelet after she saw it."

"You wore it so she would see it. You put this in action. It was all for you, not for her."

"Whatever, Destiny."

"Maybe Audrey is different," she continues. "I hope she is. But I need to set DJ free. It feels greedy that I kept him this close this long."

"He wants to be with you forever," I point out.

"He wants to be with *Destiny* forever."

"Well, yeah. I mean, can't he at least have another year or something? Why rush?"

Destiny falls quiet.

And it clicks. Holy batballs! She's considering *not* picking Destiny. The notion takes me aback. I guess I'd assumed all year that she'd choose to be Destiny. I mean, I would. Anyone in their right mind would. Look at her. Look at how people treat her. Why not go through life like that if you have the chance?

"You aren't declaring Destiny?" I ask, incredulous.

"I don't know," she admits after a breath. "I don't know what I'm doing. What I do know is that I don't want to be thinking about a guy while I'm supposed to be thinking about ME, about who I'm trying to be."

"You sound like a Mary J. Blige song."

"Let me guess, one of your mom's playlists?" she asks, switching it up, done with the combative part of the conversation, holding up a thick notebook with *V1* printed on the front. "These Chronicles, man. They mess with your head."

"I can't even imagine what reading those feels like."

"Well, you will soon enough," she says, dropping the notebook, part one of four years' worth of Destiny's every thought and feeling thudding on her desk.

"What's the worst stuff to read so far?" I ask.

"Oh easy, my time with you."

"Ha ha."

"You'll be at my Forever Ceremony next week, right?" she asks genuinely.

"Wouldn't miss it."

"Wait—duh, you *have* to be there," she says. "Changers Council rules! All Y-3s have to see what the Forever Ceremony's all about so you know what to expect next year."

"I'd come even if Turner wasn't taking attendance."

"Honest, I'm happy you'll be there when I declare," she says, gesturing to the stack of Chronicles on her desk. "I guess I gotta get back to these."

"If there's anything I can do to help, holla. I can point out the pros and cons of your various personality traits—"

"There is one thing," she cuts in. "I'm going to write DJ a letter. A real-life old-fashioned paper one with a feather quill and ink and all that—and I want you to give it to him before my ceremony."

"Done. Maybe use a regular pen though."

"I love you, Kimmie. You feel that, right?"

"I love you too," I say, adding, "but only if you pick Destiny!"

At that she made a grotesque face, contorting her lips and nose into unnerving shapes, right up close to the camera on her laptop, before she hung up.

She was still pretty.

KIM

CHANGE 3-DAY 275

Central Graduation was today. I couldn't sit next to Audrey because she was with her family, her parents shedding copious tears when Jason limped across stage in his thick ankle boot and wooted as he reached center stage. I was there to support DJ and, let's be real, spend as much time as possible in Audrey's vicinity before she's shipped off to orthodox redneck camp.

Luckily, I sat where I could see Audrey and she could see me—a direct line, in fact. It was so sunny we both wore sunglasses, but a tingle still went up my spine when I sensed her gazing my way, that sweet smile on her face, those glossy pink lips. I swear she was just about to melt my insides to liquid, when I heard DJ's name announced from the loudspeaker.

I hopped up from my seat, clapped and whistled as he received his diploma and shook the principal's hand (even though they announced you're not supposed to do that for individual students). Whatevs. Give me detention next year; I'll definitely show up!

I whistled even louder when DJ turned and waved at his family in the middle rows, the sound startling and loud enough that even DJ heard, grinning and pointing my way before exiting stage left. After graduation, I "met" DJ's mom Emebet, and by "met" I mean reintroduced myself as Kim, since we of course met when I was Oryon and she drove us to the Youth Poetry Slam finals that DJ dominated last year. As proud as Emebet was then, she was one hundred times prouder today, beaming and telling everyone within a mile radius that her baby boy was going to Yale!

When she asked me and DJ to get together and pose for a photo, DJ whispered through his smile, "What did Destiny say?"

To which I answered through an equally clenched smile, "One sec."

"Say *Yale*!" his mom commanded.

"Yaaaaaaaale!" SNAP.

DJ and I huddled. I reached into my rear pocket and pulled out an envelope, passing it to him and squeezing his hand when he took it.

"I'm the proverbial messenger. Don't shoot!"

"So, not good news then," he mumbled.

"She really loves you," I said. "Maybe read it later?"

He nodded and hugged me hard before being dragged away for yet more photos with yet another batch of delighted relatives. At which point I spotted Audrey across the field going through the same family-portrait rigmarole, although in a decidedly less heartwarming environment.

"Smile, little lady!" I heard her mother demand, as Audrey stood beside Jason, who was pretending to hump his empty diploma holder, because of course he was short the credits needed to graduate. "Jason Beauregard! You stop being so silly," his mom said, as he struck a Heisman Trophy pose in his robe, then pretended to run and block Audrey on the football field.

Poor Audrey.

I got out my cell and texted her: *5 min by my scooter?*

I waited till I saw her check her phone and glance around before typing back: *I have to go to brunch at Eat-aly. Then I'm all yours.*

Me: *ALL mine?*

Audrey: *Stop it.*

Me: *I'll pick you up outside Eat-aly in 2 hours. Bring me a breadstick.*

Audrey: *xoxo*

Most excruciating two hours of my year as Kim, which was already wall-to-wall excruciating, truth be told. But that's not important anymore. I won Audrey back, and this time she's not going away, even if I am.

I can't believe it was three years ago that Audrey pressed that Snoopy wrapping paper–covered box with the silver bracelet and the drum kit charm into my hand and told me we'd be best friends forever. In fact, we were supposed to have been adding charms to the bracelet each year of our friendship, which didn't happen (for obvious reasons).

But wait, it can! I realize. So I motor over to the jewelry store next to ReRunz to see if they have any charms I can add to the bracelet, and then I can regift it to Audrey as a tangible promise of our future together.

I park, then push through the jewelry store door, which dings with an antique bell tied to the top. I scan the glass cases, searching for the charm section.

The saleslady comes over. "Do you need some help, miss?"

"I'm searching for something to go on this," I say, pulling the bracelet out.

She bends down, unlocks the cabinet, and presents a massive display case with at least a hundred velvet cubbies with silver charms in each. Jackpot.

There are windmills, an open book, a penguin, a horse, a British telephone booth, every letter of the alphabet. A popsicle. I stick my fingers into as many of the compartments as possible, dangle each charm and consider whether it's right. A tree. Interesting: life, growth, strength in the roots. Maybe. I lay it out on the counter.

A tire. No.

A flower. Her beauty. No, cheesy.

A shovel. Symbolizing my willingness to go deep with her. *Or* the holes I keep digging for myself. Pass.

A Scottie dog. Cute, but what does it mean?

Fishing rod—no. Football—hell naw. Notebook—nope. Pretzel—WTF? Who knew how many types of charms there are in the world? (Who knew people loved pretzels that much?)

Wait, what's this? A paddle-wheel riverboat. *Boom.* The boat we watched slowly putter by from the riverbank when we, uh, reconnected. Perfect. I put it on the glass countertop. "This one for sure," I say to the clerk, then keep sorting.

The Eiffel Tower. Nope. The moon. Not quite right. An anchor. Almost, maybe too cliché; lay it out. A music note, because she makes my heart sing . . . and now I'm making myself puke. And then, YES! There it is. An old-fashioned airplane like the one that was circling above when Audrey and Oryon kissed on the blanket by the community airport.

I ask the saleswoman to add the boat and plane to the bracelet beside the drum kit. But it still feels spare. I open my wallet to see how much cash I have left over from allowance.

"How much are the letters?"

"Five apiece," she says, "but if you buy three, you get one free."

"I'll take an A, D, O, and K."

"Most folks get one letter, for their first or their last name."

"I'm not most folks."

"Seems odd is all," she pushes, really leaning into her role as the bracelet police. "Unless they're the initials of your kids. They your kids?"

"I'm sixteen years old."

The saleslady just slow-blinks. "Will that do it for today?" she asks at last.

"For today," I nod, thinking about next year, and what initial I'll be coming back to buy.

After getting the charm bracelet squared away and polished up, I fill up the tank on my scooter and scoop Audrey up from behind Eat-aly, and off we go. No maps on our phones, no plan. I did hear a stern, "Be back by seven thirty!" from Audrey's father waft from around the corner of the restaurant entrance where I was hiding out. (I still keep my distance from her family, especially after the RaChas march.)

It's amazing how soon you can get out of town when you want to. How quickly the buildings get more squat, more sparse, more alike. How the cars change from foreign to American, sedans and coupes to pickups and trucks. How a rebel flag will pop up here and there, sun-faded and whipping in the wind. How the people seem less on the move, more set in their ways. Because they are. If the looks we get at the Quickie Mart are any indication.

While Audrey goes to the bathroom, I wander the aisles and pick out a couple bottles of water, some spicy chips, corn nuts, a box of Junior Mints. The guy behind the counter in a *Don't Mess with Dixie* hat sneers at me, glancing out at my Vespa, our two sparkly helmets perched on the rearview mirrors, then back at me, down at my chest. *My chest!* Then finally back up at my actual face, though he can't seem to keep his focus there.

"Eight fifty-eight," he says, with about as much disdain as can be mustered for mere numbers.

"Hey," Audrey says, bumping my hips with hers as she joins me at the counter.

The guy takes my ten-dollar bill, being sure not to touch my fingers, and sneers at Audrey, turns his back to us, muttering.

"Really?" Audrey whispers, loud enough for him to hear. I nudge her to quit.

"We're out of pennies," he spits, turning around to dump the change into my palm, again making sure we have no accidental human-to-human contact, lest he actually touch me and catch, what, feminism?

"Thank you!" Audrey says brightly (fakely), and we push through the glass door, the squeak of the hinge shy of making enough noise to drown out the "See you next Tuesday" aimed at our backs as we leave.

"Wait, did he call us—?" Audrey asks outside, seemingly ready to go back in and confront the guy.

"It's not worth it," I say. "Come on."

Audrey's face flares red, like a tomato about to burst. I feel responsible. The reality of me and what I am on the outside slamming full speed and face-first into our otherwise perfect afternoon, even though I know it's not me, it's the culture around us that's the problem.

"What a creep," she says. "I mean, why is he even . . ."

"I'm sure he has some very fine qualities," I try. "He's probably really good at Bananagrams."

Audrey rolls her eyes. Softening.

"I bet he makes an incredible tofu stir fry," I add.

"I bet he is awesome at recommending poetry," she joins, relenting.

"And dance clubs."

"And dancing."

"I bet he can do the whip like a mofo!"

And then we're off again, Audrey's arms wrapped around my waist as we fly down the street with the hot air blowing in and around our bodies, weaving through the countryside, my Vespa's throttle all the way open, us pulling almost fifty on a tiny road to wherever. I don't care. Audrey doesn't seem to either.

After about fifteen more miles, I spot a small wooden sign for a nature preserve and pull off the road, Audrey's grip around me tightening. I glance down and see the bracelet making a bump in my jeans pocket. I roll under the shade of a big willow tree, the tips of its branches overhanging a creek in this quiet little cove. There's a wooden bench facing the water. Nobody else around, save for a tiny lone figure on the other side of the river, walking away from us, a black-and-white dog bounding through the reeds.

We take off our helmets and prop them on the mirrors, and Audrey scrunches down her pants which had ridden up during the ride.

"Are you okay?" I ask, already sensing the answer.

"Mostly," she responds.

"Want to sit?" I gesture toward the weathered bench, names and initials carved into its entire surface, on every side of every slat.

She nods and sits, gazing out over the water.

"I'm really sorry that happened," I say, about being lesbian-profiled at the gas station.

"Why are *you* apologizing?"

"I don't know."

"It's not your fault," she says.

"Not in the meta sense. But I doubt he would have called you a name or acted so bothered if I'd been some white dude."

Silence. After a while, the person and dog across the river disappear around the bend.

"The world sucks," she says after a minute. "It shouldn't matter what you are or not. If you were some Abercrombie model–looking dude, that hate would still exist—if not directed at us, then at somebody else. The next couple to pull into that gas station. It's like there is a hate set point, like the water table, and there will always be a certain amount on hand, sloshing around and spilling all over certain people. I mean, history is rife with hate."

"It's also rife with grace and kindness," I counter, half-believing myself. "And not for nothing, that's why we Changers exist. To lower the levels. To reduce the slosh."

"Really worked out at the Quickie Mart."

"Yeah, well. That guy may be beyond my reach."

"I'm sorry, I'm just dreading going back to camp tomorrow. Most of the people there think like that guy at the station."

"Is there any way you can get out of it?" I ask, fingers crossed.

"I've tried. Like the last two summers—well, I mean, Drew knew. I mean . . . You know what I mean."

She laughs, but then staunches it self-consciously. "My parents made a deal with me: if I go to camp every summer, they'll help me pay for college. And I don't want to mess with that. Because I am getting the hell out of here."

I feel the bracelet pushing against my leg in my pocket.

"What's that?" Audrey asks, clued in to my distraction.

"What?" I stall.

"In your pocket. I've been wondering all day."

"Oh, this?" I say, lifting my hips and reaching into my pants, digging out a red velvety bag cinched shut with a drawstring. I place it on her thigh. "Open it."

When Audrey pulls the bracelet out of the bag, she immediately starts weeping. Says it's the most romantic thing anybody has ever done for her. How she'll wear it every day until it disintegrates around her wrist. She asks me to help her put it on, then kisses me unself-consciously, as if the gas station incident never happened.

"It's the story of us," she says, getting it instantly.

"After school starts," I say, my voice warbly, "I'll bring you the last initial to add to make it complete."

Audrey's smile is so big, so genuine, so hopeful and trusting and certain—I never want it to dissipate. She cocks her head at me. "Are you nervous?"

"About?"

"About the change."

"Should I be?"

She doesn't hesitate: "No. I'll love you no matter what."

SUMMER

KIM

CHANGE 3-DAY 276

A Changer Council Forever Ceremony is basically an *American Idol* finale, if *American Idol* had 1/100th the budget and was produced by a well-meaning cult. It's as if Turner the Lives Coach got a memo that to stay hip with the kids there needed to be flashing lights, booming bass, and outfits like you'd see at Epcot Center. (No doubt Tracy's influence there.)

Held in the large warehouse auditorium at Changers Central, the ceremony opens with the Parade of the Undeclared, all the Y-4 Changers-in-waiting wearing only black except for a white sash knotted at the hip. Turner is, of course, dressed in flowing scarlet robes and a bejeweled headdress like he's a geisha from *Big Trouble in Little China* (Mom's favorite movie that she makes me watch every year for her birthday. That Kurt Russell has a hold on her I don't care to dwell on).

I'd love nothing more than to snap a picture of this whole variety show to send to Kris, but of course cameras are forbidden at the Forever Ceremony, and Kris knows nothing of Changers, nor how he essentially is one without actually being one, so sharing this particular absurdity will have to wait until Changers are completely out in the open, and a hundred-year-old Ryan Seacrest wheels out onstage to host the televised version of Forever Ceremonies for the whole world to tune in and TEXT THEIR VOTE! for which V each Y-4 Changer should pick.

After a few introductory videos about how great the hopefully-not-too-distant future will one day be, Turner slinks up to center stage and starts speaking. It's the usual *In the many, we are one* groupthink, a version of what we hear every year at the first Changers Mixer of whatever V you've changed into, but with a few added flourishes for the special occasion of all these Y-4 Changers on the brink of completing their Cycles and selecting their Forever V's. Macaroni-and-cheesy though it is, it can't help but feel monumental.

"When you become the image of your own imagination, it's the most powerful thing you could ever do," Turner thunders, after which I reflexively tune out; I strain my head and squint to see if I can spot where Destiny is sitting in the front row. As Turner carries on (various words and phrases manage to penetrate my consciousness—"chosen," "mission," "gift you've been given," "model for your people," "exponential growth"—a few parents begin to snuffle and root tissues from their pockets. And then, finally, the first of half a dozen or so Y-4 Changers from the Southeastern region walks up to announce who he will be for the rest of his life.

Immediately I'm consumed with the sheer terror of recognition that I'll have to do this myself in a year's time. I guess all Turner's blather is kind of astute: we are watching nothing less than the birth of a generation. And the heaviness of choosing one iteration, at the expense of three others, is powerful, but also heartbreaking. How do you say goodbye forever to yourselves?

The first Y-4 stands nervously beside the podium, like he is unsure where to go, even though I know there had to be at least three rehearsals for the ceremony prior to this moment. Turner sidles over, grips the kid's shoulder, and nods for him to step forward and speak. Photos of all four of his V's flash theatrically on the screen behind him, one after the other, as he searches the crowd and lands on his parents, who clap sparsely for a few rounds before the whole audience joins in applauding encouragement to spur the kid to embrace his moment.

"Always hardest to go first," Turner says performatively into the flesh-colored microphone headset pressed to his cheek.

The kid anxiously low-talks a few words about his four-year journey, then, fast as he can, presses one of four buttons atop the podium, as a soft, ancient-sounding drumbeat begins to pulse through the room. The lights dim, a cone of spotlight on him while he slowly turns his back to the audience and peers up at the four photos on the screens above; in the last he is his current V, of course, a skinny white kid who looks like the fifth Beatle. He bows his head, and the lights cut out suddenly and entirely, where all we can see are the images of the four V's projected on one giant screen.

One by one they go dark. Until the only one left illuminated is his V from junior year, Vincent, a handsome black guy with Colin Kaepernick hair and wearing a bright-red T-shirt. The lights come back, and the graduate spins around, but now he's that guy. The whole room cheers, a few people shouting his chosen name. Vincent embraces Turner and a few other berobed Changers Council members, before shakily returning to his seat in the first row.

It's intimate and emotional and more than a little mind-blowing that the Y-4s are changing onstage like a Criss Angel mindfreak magic trick, but I'm holding it down.

A few more graduates go, then finally it's Destiny's turn. We watch the montage of her V's populate the screens, and I have to say, it's trippy as hell to see her as Tapia and Colton, her first two V's I never knew, nor heard much about. It dawns on me right then that not everybody gets two girls and two boys as their V's; Elyse got three girls and one boy (and was a boy before she turned into Tapia).

Then a photo of Elyse comes up on the screens—my cellmate and recovery buddy, and the kind of badass chick we all aspire to be, no matter what our outside gender. Before I can get too misty missing Elyse, a photo of Destiny pops up, and I swear you can hear a collective gasp from the audience, like Beyoncé burst into the room in a sparkle leotard or something. The photo of Destiny lingers, eating up the screen with so much organic glamour and charm it makes your head spin, and it's obvious to everybody in the joint what Destiny's destiny is.

Real-life Destiny approaches the podium, bumping the mic with her chin as she leans in, causing a jolt of feedback, and it's probably the only time I've seen her seem outwardly nervous in a year. She apologizes for the disturbance, clears her throat in a sweet little hiccup, and bends the stem of the mic toward her perfect lips. The room is silent, rapt.

"Voltaire wrote, *Minds differ still more than faces,*" she begins. "One thing I've realized over my short lives is that no matter who we are or who we become, our time is limited. So there's no use wasting even a minute of it living someone else's life. As I've inhabited these four bodies, and especially while rereading my Chronicles, it's become clearer that of those four lives you see onscreen, only one of them has made me truly feel like I was alive, like I was myself."

Destiny is calm while she speaks these words, but I can tell she's choking down a sizable lump in her throat. I scooch forward in my seat, as if that half-inch will make a difference and I'll hear the news quicker.

"One of the hardest lessons I've struggled to learn over the last four years is not to let others' opinions drown out my inner voice and intuition. But in this instance, the biggest one we'll face as Changers, I have decided to follow my heart."

And at that, Destiny reaches to press her button on the podium, the drumbeat commencing, the spotlight on her while she turns her back, bows her head. Again, the lights cut, and one by one her photos go dark. First Tapia, then Colton . . . and then the last . . .

Destiny.

Leaving only my friend, my dear, special friend: Elyse.

The lights snap back up, and Elyse turns around to face us, the audience erupting in celebration as they have for each new Mono. I am straight-up bawling, so thrilled to see Elyse again. I wasn't sure I ever would.

It's not that I didn't adore Destiny. Destiny was an undeniable force of wonder and beauty. But she wasn't Elyse. Or more, as Destiny's speech made clear, Elyse *wasn't* Destiny.

I guess Destiny was sort of like a boss cocktail dress that you wear out on special occasions, pose for the cat-calling paparazzi, then go home and peel off because the straps are cutting into your shoulder blades. Whereas Elyse was goofy pajamas and prescription eyeglasses and fly-away hair. And the kind of confidence that doesn't come from the outside. Elyse was . . . Elyse. And Elyse choosing Elyse says more about her essential Elyse-ness than anything else. She picked the awkward weirdo, the tougher row. She opted to be seen by the few, not worshipped by the many. She made a choice I'm not sure many people would, Changers or Statics, if they had the chance.

I mean, damn, who doesn't want to be Beyoncé?

Elyse. That's who. God, I love that girl.

In the seat next to me, my mom sees the tears streaming down my face and pulls me tight under her arm, kissing me lightly on the head. I feel exposed, but I can't seem to stop. The naked emotion of Elyse declaring herself overriding all my cynicism and the silliness of the ceremony and Turner's stupid, drapey robes.

The lights come up on the whole room. Elyse accepts Turner's embrace, shaking a few more Changers Council hands, gingerly stepping offstage. I can see she is also crying, but smiling too, grinning ear to ear, unburdened, flooded with the palpable joy that comes from finally seeing yourself the way you always imagined you would be.

Turner wrapped up the ceremony with a few words aimed especially at the Y-3s in the house, advising us to live our last approaching V's to the fullest and Chronicle our hearts out, because we will be called up to this stage to declare before we know it. Noted.

Afterward, I made my way to Elyse and we hugged for a brief moment, held on tight—but it was her Forever Ceremony, and all the Monos were swept up with family and Touchstones, and one-on-one powwows with Turner about their new, refocused responsibilities as they enter the world, I'm sure referencing the eventual goal (no rush though!) to find Static mates, and be a vessel to help spread the gospel of empathy and change. (A message that never stops feeling a tad Big Brother-y to me, but hey, not the time or the place for resistance.)

Elyse promised she'd get in touch as soon as she could, but I knew there was going to be tons for her to do in the next months. Orientation sessions and meetings at Changers Central, the arranging of college admissions, potential relocations, beginning the process of blending past lives with this new/old forever one.

As my dad said goodbye to a few of the Council members, my mom put her arm around my waist and we headed toward the bright sunlight streaming through the glass in the lobby. I turned and gave Elyse one last wave and a big thumbs-up, like everything was aca-awesome. But of course it wasn't. Not entirely. The Forever Ceremony is uplifting and inspiring and full-circley and all that, but it is also a stark reminder that the great big final unknown is coming for me yet again.

In a mere two and a half months, Kim (like Ethan, Drew, and Oryon before her) will be chucked to the curb with last week's recycling, and I will awake as someone new.

And unlike Elyse, I don't even have a gut feeling as to where I'm leaning as far as declaring my Mono. It seems like I should have a sense of growing conviction like she did, or a tingling like Tracy always describes it, that someone I've lived as either IS or ISN'T who I "essentially" am.

But I don't.

Drew, Oryon, Kim, they all kind of feel like me—but also *don't* feel like me. I'm sure that's some fundamental failing on my part. I mean, that was the message hammered home in so many different ways at the ceremony, by Council leadership, by every Y-4 Changer who stepped up on that stage and spoke their truth: *Don't worry what others think; worry what* you *think.*

Destiny made the choice for her to be Elyse, despite the fact that DJ of course would (obviously) prefer Destiny. I mean, had she given him a chance, maybe he would choose otherwise, but she let go entirely of what he might or might not do, and made the decision that was right for her. Me? I can't stop agonizing over how Audrey will feel about the next me. Whether she'll be able to live with him/her/them for a year, whether she'll be able to love them like she promises she will, like she loved Drew and Oryon before.

I want to believe her. But deep down, it's impossible to truly predict how you will feel about something that hasn't even happened yet. Trust me on that. I'm kind of an expert.

KIM

CHANGE 3-DAY 348

Herewith: the sum of my summer, conveniently bullet-pointed for (my own) future reference ...

- Working six days a week at ReRunz, sometimes seven when this skuzzy yet still appealing Changer guy named Tiq bails on account of staying out too late drinking and smoking with his equally skuzzy (less appealing) buddies, then calls me last minute to fill in for him because he's "way too hungover to fold clothes."
- Paying for gas, insurance, and significant mechanical and cosmetic repairs on my Vespa, in preparation for all the places I plan to take Audrey with me once school starts.
- Walking Andy through Destiny's decision not to be Destiny, at least once and sometimes twice a day.
- Balancing on the friendship tightrope with Kris, who I want to confide in, but thanks to then-Destiny's lecture about burdening your loved ones with the truth, I have decided I probably can't. So trying to enjoy what little time I have left with him as Kim and hoping he gets sidetracked

by his own mini-dramas, of which there are plenty.

- Going vegetarian (in Audrey's honor), then going back to eating turkey and chicken, then going vegetarian again—before finally going back to eating everything because at the end of every shift at Sweet Melissa's Chicken Shack where Andy works, we can cop as much free food as we can stuff our faces with.

- Seeing Tracy for an awkward afternoon tea, during which she apologized for letting me down by seemingly giving up on me after the RaChas march, and insisting that no matter what I do, or how frustrated she gets, she will never actually give up on me. And let's not forget her making me promise not to tell Audrey who I am next year, so that it limits the exposure I brought on ALL OF US by participating in the RaChas action and tipping off Audrey to the fact that Changers might exist (if she only knew half of what I actually shared with Audrey).

- Going on a quick beach weekend in Florida with my mom, dad, and Andy, during which it rained the whole time, and some kid got a superficial shark bite on the shin where we were staying, so rain or shine you were not going to find my chubby butt bobbing out in that water like so much *Jaws* bait. We did connect with one of Nana's friends from her old apartment complex, who gave me a box of Nana's things that had been left behind when Mom and Dad moved her in with us earlier this year. They still smelled like Nana.

- Awaiting a much-anticipated yet ultimately aborted Facetime from Audrey, who texted in the middle of the night on July 4 that she was going to be able to escape her camp for an hour and wanted to connect, but then her call never came.

- DJ rolling by ReRunz to say goodbye to me before his mom drove him up to Connecticut for school, where he was enrolled in a special pre-college program and had a part-time campus job waiting for him. He was still sort of smarting from never getting to actually lay eyes on Destiny again, but I'm not worried about DJ—he's going to thrive in the Ivy League. And Yale's going to be better for having him there. Way better.

- Setting aside especially fly wardrobe selections that come through ReRunz for my future self, even though I have no idea what size, color, style, or vibe that might need to be. Much less gender. But then, I've kind of let go of the whole dressing-for-your-gender thing. What a racket that is.

- Stopping by the jewelry store to keep an eye on the charms they have available. It appears they have run out of the letters T, L, and X, so here's to praying my new name isn't going to be Tiger, Lola, or Xander.

- And finally, only last week, another peculiar tea with Tracy, and this time Mr. Crowell too, during which they announced they were going to have a baby, and before I could even have a reaction, Tracy immediately set in, assuring me (even though I didn't need it) that newborn or no, she would never be distracted from her duties as my Touchstone, and that yes, *technically* Touchstones are supposed to hold off on reproducing until after their Changer charges have completed their Cycle, but that things went super-duper fast and they were so excited to get their lives started that they decided they could handle it, no problem. "So it was an accident?" I asked, while Tracy was horrified that I even knew how babies were made, and Mr. Crowell said, "Basically, yes."

KIM

CHANGE 3-DAY 362

T-minus three days.

Approximately thirty hours until IT happens again. *Woo.*

The only cold comfort being that this is the last time I will have a night like the one coming up in three days, hardcore fretting over who the hell I'm going to be when I wake up the next morning.

Mom and Dad are walking around with permanent proud-of-me anticipatory faces, and I keep hearing rumblings about Dad beginning to enter the selection process to become an official member of the Changers Council. Fun times. As if I don't already feel pressure to be the model Changer child.

We finally got Andy's transcripts sent from New York, plus reluctant permission from his father, so he's going to enroll at Central when I do, repeating his junior year which he never completed back home, seeing as he ran away.

But most of all: Audrey is back from camp, and said we can meet up on the day before school starts. I am ecstatic to see her.

KIM

CHANGE 3-DAY 365

"**S**o you wake up and then find out who you are from your parents or something?" Audrey asks me over dip cones at the Freezo. "What happens exactly?"

"I don't even really know," I whisper through frozen lips, whipping my head around to make sure we're not being watched by her brother or other Abider goons.

"Do you feel it when it's happening?"

"Ish."

"I'm getting a sense you don't want to talk about it," Audrey says, licking chocolate drips off the side of her cone.

"It's, well, I'm not really supposed—"

"Cool, cool, I don't need to pry."

I lean back and eye Audrey, am reminded how I promised her honesty. And how there's no such thing as half-honesty.

"Okay, so," I start, realizing this is the first time I've talked about this process with a Static besides my mother. "The night before, well, *tonight*, before I go to sleep, I'll feel kind of anxious—"

"Obviously!" Audrey breaks in.

"More anxious than usual," I say. "And I'll spare you the details of what races through my head, but I basically feel as if I'm coming down with a cold, and then once I finally do fall asleep, despite trying not to, so as to stave off the change—believe me, I've tried that and it doesn't work—I sleep really, really deeply, and when I wake up I'm a new person."

"Wow."

"Yeah, wow."

"I mean, like, WOW."

By now it seems somewhat "normal" to me, or at least my norm, but I realize staring into Audrey's screwed-up-but-trying-to-remain-open face, it isn't.

"So you, so, so . . ."

"Are you done with that?" I ask, pointing to the bottom, the best part, of her cone. She hands it over. "Remember the Bickersons song 'The Bottom Is the Tastiest Bit'?"

I serenade Audrey, come to think of it, in the same booth Chase and I last sat in before he—well, died. What a trip this life is. These lives are. Each and every one of them. I kind of wish I believed in the whole dead-people-watching-us-thing. Wonder what Chase would be thinking. If he'd be proud of me. Maybe. Probably not.

"Do you sleep naked?" Audrey blurts.

"That's personal," I say, feigning modesty. "But no."

"Me neither."

Audrey giggles, and I join in. After the ice cream is gone, she glances at her phone for about the fourth time.

"Got somewhere to be?" I ask. "I can drop you on the scooter."

"No, that's good. I'm waiting for a ride." Her demeanor has changed. And I recognize it.

"Who's coming to get you?"

She cuts her eyes in my direction.

"I thought he was going to college," I whine.

She shakes her head, stares at the ground. "He deferred because of his knee. He's staying here and assistant-coaching the football team while he rehabs."

I can't believe what I'm hearing. I thought we'd finally be free of the wrath of Jason, the trapped hair in the drain no one wants to pick out.

"Neat," I say with maximum sarcasm.

"Yeah, *neat*," Audrey echoes, checking her phone again. "I got my license this summer, but I need a job to pay for a car."

I decide I'm not going to waste the last seconds I have with Audrey talking about her missing-link brother.

"Whatever, we will persevere!" I announce. "But this means you have to go? I was hoping we could take a walk down by the river."

I wink, but Audrey's not having it. I go around and sit next to her in the booth, put my arm around her. I don't care who sees. She feels smaller than usual, but I scoot in close, push the hair behind her ear, and give her a kiss on the cheek.

"*I will always love you,*" I sing, Dolly-style.

At that Audrey's cheeks flush pink, and she grins. I want to kiss her so bad, like really kiss her, but already the parents of the Lands' End catalog–model family in the booth across from us are shifting in their seats, distracting the kids from glancing our way with whatever's flashing on the iPad propped on the table. Talk about family values.

The familiar Mustang horn sounds out front, jarring us both, and I immediately spot Jason through the window, wearing his old Central jersey with the sleeves cut off. And he spots me. I smile right at him.

"I'll see you in the morning," I say to Audrey, and watch her go for the last time with Kim's eyes.

FALL

CHANGE 4-DAY 1

I'm scared. Really scared.

I lied to everybody today.

Mom, Dad, Tracy, they all think I enrolled at Central like usual, obediently went off to school like a good Y-4 Changer.

Andy thinks that too, although he was a little suspicious when I begged off before we got to campus this morning, saying I'd catch up with him at lunch. Which I never did. Because I never went to campus.

I'm seriously thinking of driving to one of the Cumberland River bridges and jumping off. But I'm afraid it wouldn't kill me. This body would survive it.

Okay. Back up.

I know all this sounds dramatic, but I don't know what to do. Don't know how else to stop the future from happening.

I'm the *Titanic*'s captain; I can see the iceberg way up ahead in the distance, and it seems like there's ample time to avoid it, to switch directions, but in fact geometry and physics and gravity are all conspiring to keep me headed straight for the massive frozen behemoth in my path. The time-space continuum won't allow me to change course. What am I going to do? Stand by the wheel and wait for the inevitable slow-speed deadly collision with destiny? Or blow up the whole damn cursed ship before it has the chance to collide?

Okay, I need to think.

I ride and ride my scooter until I find a coffee shop I've never been to, in East Nashville. There's no chance of running into anybody I know. Not that they'd recognize me.

Think, think.

There's a bridge a five-minute walk from here. If I had enough courage, I'd do it. Chase sacrificed for me. Why shouldn't I for Audrey?

I should probably rewind: When I woke up this morning, I had a Destiny moment. As in, waking up in a body and as a person the whole world will, if not love, give a cultural privilege pass to, finally. FINALLY.

When Andy came in to use the bathroom, he caught me hoisting my shirt and staring at my abs in the full-length mirror behind the door.

"Holy shit, man," he said, his pupils wide as dinner plates.

"I know." I dropped the shirt back over my ripped stomach.

"I mean, this is some weird science up in here. Talk about before-and-after pictures."

"I can't really digest it myself," I said, awed.

"I suggest quitting high school and moving to Europe to model."

"So I'm Zoolander now?" I asked.

"You're not *not* Zoolander, bro."

I couldn't stop double-checking myself in the mirror. I was basically the missing Hemsworth brother. About six feet, muscles for days, bright-blue eyes, a killer smile, perfect floppy sandy-blond hair (but not too floppy), high cheek-bones, thick brows.

"Does this mean you're going to be stuffing me into lockers and dumpsters now?" Andy asked, dropping trou and stepping into the steamy shower. (Something, by the way, he NEVER would've done merely the night before, when I was Kim and we were sharing the same tiny bath-room. How quickly behavior changes when gender does.)

As soon as I returned to my bedroom, Mom came in. She peered UP at me, as in way up, craning her neck (maybe I'm taller than six feet), and couldn't contain her smile. I hugged her, her head barely hitting my pecs. My consider-able, ridiculous pecs.

"Well, this is going to be quite a year," she pronounced, stepping back and taking a long gander at me, eyes boggling like Andy's had. "Lot of facial symmetry going on." (Mom's way of calling me conventionally attractive without betray-ing her feminist roots.)

Then my dad poked his head in, followed by Snoopy. The room felt crowded. "Nice one," Dad said, fist-bumping me. He couldn't contain his pride, even though he was offi-cially supposed to. All V's are viewed as equal in *The Chang-ers Bible*. Not in the real world, of course. Or even in this bedroom, apparently.

"Take that, Abiders!" he shouted, meaning, presumably, that I was finally a worthy adversary to our mortal enemies.

Mom threw the new V packet from the Changers Council on my bed. "Tracy's stopping by in a few; tell Andy breakfast will be ready when he gets out of the shower."

After a few more lingering appraisals, Mom and Dad

left, and I was alone in my room, Andy singing Led Zeppelin in the shower, loud enough for me to hear: "*In the days of my youth I was told what it means to be a man . . .*" He was really pouring it on thick and rich.

Idling there on my own, except for Snoopy (who even seemed like a smaller dog to me now), I was almost nervous being around myself. The way I always get nervous around really attractive people. Except this time *I* was the really attractive person. This was going to take some getting used to. Not that I was complaining.

Reminded that there was a backstory to this guy I was abruptly inhabiting, that he has some insides in addition to these outsides, I picked up the packet, unstrung the fastener, and slid out the thick file.

Right across the top, in bold black and white . . . my name.

My NAME?

I can't even say it. Can't even think it.

———

KYLE.

KYLE

CHANGE 4-DAY 1, PART TWO

I find myself perched on the bridge, a couple feet east of the center. Downtown to the right, East Nashville to my left. I put both hands on the guardrail, lean way over the edge, and crane almost under the bridge. It seems farther down than I thought it would. The water is brown and dirty, way less scenic than upriver where Audrey and I . . . Oh god.

Kyle.

Kyle. Kyle. Kyle.

This can't be happening.

I'm the guy from the vision. The kiss vision I had with Audrey.

I'm the guy I've been paranoid about, keeping my eye out for ever since Audrey and I kissed on the dance floor at prom freshman year, when Audrey surprised the crap out of me and in the presence of every single person at prom leaned in and planted one on me with her perfect soft lips—and the world disappeared for a few seconds.

Until the flash of Audrey's future. Audrey sitting in a car screaming, enraged to the point of tears, her face red and damp. Fighting with a big, athletic, movie star–looking guy leaning through the window. Kyle. *Me.*

In the vision, he's (I'm?) grabbing her arm, trying to snatch the key so she can't drive off, but Audrey pushes him/

me away and yells, "I hate you, Kyle!" before punching the gas and speeding off ... And then a distant CRASH.

In the vision I can see it unfold in slow motion, Audrey T-boned by that speeding delivery truck in the distance. There is smoke, the beginnings of flames, the horn blowing nonstop, like something—or someone—is lying across it.

Then the vision ends.

I feel my leg twitch, and without me really even controlling what's happening, I feel it lift up onto the lower rail and I begin an instinctive climb that feels almost like second nature to this body. My hands squeeze the railing, sweating on the hot metal. I have no control over my muscles, and I'm not sure I want to ... but—

"Hey!"

—

"Hey!" It's a lady's voice coming from somewhere behind me. "Sir, are you okay?"

I glance right, where an old cream-colored Volvo is pulled to the side of the bridge, hazard lights on, the passenger door flung open. The driver, a middle-aged woman with salt-and-pepper hair and wearing yoga garb, is walking toward me with a sense of urgency. I still don't know exactly what I'm doing, why she's coming toward me with her hands outstretched.

"Can you do me a favor, son?" she says calmly, arriving right behind me, but keeping her distance. "Can you step down off that railing and talk to me for a little bit? I won't take much of your time."

She has the most homey Southern drawl you've ever heard, right out of a Hallmark movie. Except it feels genuine.

Something clicks in my brain, and I'm newly aware of both my feet on the lower rail, my hands on the upper, me bent in half, stretching toward the water below. I could release at any time, and I'd be free-falling in a blink.

"Son, I really could use your help with something down here," she says.

I inch back and instantly feel the woman's hands on my calves, guiding my feet to the concrete. Once they're firmly on the ground, I turn. Her eyes are kind, with wrinkles fanning the edges.

"Thank you," she says, taking my hand.

I can't say anything.

"Let's you and me go have a seat in the car over here," she suggests, and starts walking, gently tugging me by the wrist.

I follow her lead like a toddler. She sits me down in the passenger side of her double-parked Volvo, my feet on the curb of the bridge.

"Is this okay?" she asks.

"I think so," I manage. A car honks at us, speeds around us. I stare at my palms. They're red, scorched from the sizzling metal of the railing.

"What say you breathe with me? Let's take three deep breaths in and out together." She takes one herself, demonstrating for me. Then counts out as I join her.

After the third deep breath, my chest feels looser.

"Now, of course I'm not in your shoes," she says then, matter-of-fact-like. "But to my thinking, there's almost nothing that can't be figured out somehow, over time."

"I don't think I was really going to do anything," I say,

suddenly flooded with first, recognition, and then, the shame of what this must look like.

"If you were or you weren't, that was then," she says, with absolutely no judgment in her voice. "And this is now, and I'm glad you're here with me now, for however long or short that lasts."

Her words make me want to curl into a ball at her feet. To spill everything about how I'm not really depressed and suicidal, that (for once) I don't hate myself or feel hopeless or just want the pain to stop. Rather, it's that if I don't kill myself, then I will likely cause the death of somebody I love more than myself. Her kindness makes me almost believe I could tell her the truth: that I'd seen the future and I'm a murderous asshole in it.

"I think I might be a bad person," I mumble after a while.

"Oh, honey, join the club," she says, waving her hand in the air. "Anyone with half a brain thinks they're awful sometimes. It's the people who don't that you've got to worry about."

I offer a thin smile.

She catches my eye. "I teach yoga at the local prison. You know who's in my class? Whole lotta men who hate themselves but can't say it. They're drinking poison and praying everyone else gets sick. I get it. But it's no long-term strategy."

I nod absently, trying to make sense of everything, of myself. Maybe I do hate myself and feel hopeless and just want the pain to stop.

"What you want to be mindful of, son, is that you don't pick a permanent solution to a temporary problem. Believe you me, everybody can change."

CHANGE 4-DAY 1, PART THREE

Dinner was complete BS, to say the least.

The main course was lying to my parents about which classes I liked, classes I didn't even attend. Then lying about my schedule, which I didn't get, and my classmates, who I didn't meet.

"Mrs. Miller, this mac 'n' cheese is amazing," Andy said, after answering Dad's fifty questions about his first day of school in Tennessee and how it differs from New York State.

"Aren't you sweet?" Mom cooed. "Did you boys see each other on campus today?"

I took advantage of Andy's full mouth. "Nope," I lied. Again.

"What are the odds of that?" Dad observed idly as Andy swallowed.

"Yeah, what are the odds?" Andy poked, being a bit of a dick. "Where'd you sit at lunch?"

I stuffed in my own huge bite of mac 'n' cheese, pretended to answer.

"Manners, Kyle," Mom chided.

"Why didn't you go to school today?" Andy presses me when he's on the way to the bathroom before going to bed on the TV room pullout couch.

"Who says I didn't?"

Andy weaves his neck like he's auditioning for *Real Housewives of Central High*. "Don't play a player, dude."

There is nothing to do but tell him. Everything. Down to the Audrey kiss vision of the car crash, courtesy of Kyle—well, me. (Not the bridge part. No one needs to know about that.) So I spill.

"Hmmm. I totally see your dilemma," Andy says when I finish. He sits back against a pillow on my bed. "But are you planning on ditching your entire senior year? You can't avoid your problems by running away from them."

"Seriously, dude? You're living in our TV room."

Andy blanches, wounded.

"I think I miss Kim," he barks. Then: "I can help keep an eye on Audrey. But maybe you should tell her the deal?"

"NOOOOO!" I yell, loud enough that Mom veers into the room while she's walking by.

"You guys okay in here?" she asks, peeking in.

"Super-duper," I say.

"Yeah, super-duper," Andy echoes, both of us coming off like jackholes.

"Well, don't stay up *super-duper* late," Mom says. "Y'all have a lot of new stuff to contend with at school, so it's best to get as much rest as possible. Keep that immunity strong!"

"Yes ma'am," Andy says. "I'll head to bed in a few minutes."

"*Ma'am?*" she teases and smiles, lingering a few extra seconds in the doorway before leaving, Mom intuition kicking in. I can tell she smells something's up with me. Hopefully she chalks it up to the usual Changer transition trauma. Same headspace, different head.

When she closes the door, I whisper to Andy, "Do NOT say anything to them. Or anyone."

"I gotchu, bro. But eventually . . ."

"I know. I know. I need time to figure it out, and I'm not going to put myself in Audrey's world until I do."

"Well, technically you're already in it."

"Shut up, Andy," I say, and we dap before he heads out to the couch, where he will presumably sleep like a baby while I lie awake searching for holes in the space-time continuum.

CHANGE 4-DAY 2

Today I "got ready for school" and left with Andy, dropping him close enough to walk but not close enough to be spotted, zipping off on my Vespa to kill time until classes ended.

I decided to catch a movie at a giant nondescript multiplex in the suburbs. The room was empty except for three other solo people, all of whom appeared also to be avoiding some aspect of their lives, some less successfully than others. I paid next to zero attention to the title of the movie when I bought a ticket; it was some action flick about a kid who's a really good driver, and for some reason is indebted to a criminal who makes the kid pilot the getaway car for the complicated robberies the guy orchestrates. It's all fun and games until people get shot.

The kid is, of course, a sad orphan. His parents died in a, wait for it, car crash when he was young, so he feels responsible and is all alone and messed up from it, hiding from the world behind hipster sunglasses and headphones—fine and dandy, but it makes me think of Audrey and the accident in the vision, and my part in it, and how I'm trying to hide from the world and my guilt and I don't even get to speed around in a cool car.

After the movie ends—he opens up and finds love but has to pay his debt to society before he can run off with that love (did I mention the TWO female characters are literally a saint and a whore?)—I realize I have four more hours until I can pick up Andy and go home. I skulk around the multi-plex, sneaking into a second theater where the latest Marvel movie is one-third of the way through. It's a bunch of mu-tants trying to save the world despite nobody really under-standing them. Not what I came for. But I watch anyway.

CHANGE 4–DAY 3

Today I decided to forgo the movie route and kill time instead by shopping at ReRunz for Kyle. Perfect Kyle, the male Destiny of V's, whom everybody else in the world flocks to, but whom I despise. Oh, what I'd do to be Kim again. Never thought I'd hear *that* thought rattling around this brain.

I don't bother trying to figure out who's who this year at ReRunz. Don't bother coming out to my boss Neal, the Changer who manages the shop. There's this understood agreement that all Changers tell Neal who they are after a new V emerges, so that we're clued into who to keep an eye out for, who are allies. But, like, why bother anymore?

Soon as I walk into the shop and smell that familiar used clothes scent, a dash of B.O. mixed with damp wool, Neal walks right up to me and asks, "Can I help you find anything?" like he's never seen me before. Which he hasn't.

I'm too messed up to give a crap what I wear, but, irony of ironies, everything I throw on looks great and feels incredible. Nothing binds or cuts or clings. It's as if each piece was sewn specifically for me.

I have a $122 credit from selling most of Kim's wardrobe, but I don't want to spend it, because then Neal would realize it's me. As I'm trying on the last pair of jeans in the back of the shop, a nice-smelling lady comes up and threads her arm between my chest and bicep. "Oooh," she murmurs, "this is definitely your style."

I instinctively flinch, obviously unused to being touched by random strangers. It's been two short days, but I'm starting to see what Destiny was talking about. All the attention and constant benefit of the doubt spurting all over me as if from a fire hose. I see why celebrities are always demanding NO EYE CONTACT! They want a freaking break from empty, unearned attraction. Look away, look away!

"Heh," I manage to grunt at this lady, who is about forty, with a ten-year-old skater kid in tow. She won't stop smiling at me.

"What's your story?" she asks, while her kid tries on a pair of used Vans.

"Excuse me?" I say, then take my clothes to the counter.

It isn't until I've paid, left the shop, and I'm throwing a leg over my scooter that I realize she was hitting on me. Like in all the teen movies where the cougar MILFs feed on dumb high school guys. Except this time I'm not playing the role of the nerdy friend whose mom is hot; I'm the dumb guy who doesn't know any better.

Later that night at home, I gather the last of Kim's stuff into a trash bag and shove it in the back of the closet, then put away my new clothes. I spot the box of Nana's belongings in the corner, and though I could really use a dose of Nana energy, it's not the right time to go through it yet. I don't want to get all emo in front of Andy, who's struggling with his math homework on my bed.

"Figure anything out?" he asks.

"Not yet."

"They're going to realize you're not in school at some point," he says, erasing something in his spiral notebook. "You don't even have books in your backpack."

"I need more time," I say. But in truth, I'm no further along "figuring this out" than I was when I woke up and realized I was Kyle. This is one of those conundrums that has no solution that doesn't involve me disappearing.

Andy scribbles a new answer where he'd erased one. "This is impossible," he announces of precalculus.

"Did you see her today?" I ask then, closing my closet and plopping down on the bed next to him.

"She was with some cheerleader chick, and a guy dressed like one of the Golden Girls," Andy says, barely paying attention.

"That was Kris. Did he seem okay?"

"How am I supposed to tell?"

"Was the girl Chloe?"

"Who's Chloe?"

"How did Audrey look?"

"How a pretty senior girl looks. Busy, closed off. Out of my league."

"Was she wearing a silver charm bracelet?" I ask.

"You mean the one from the sorcerer on the mountain that holds all the witchy spells?"

"Come on."

"I don't know!" he says, exasperated.

"Okay, but did she seem especially upset or concerned or—"

"Dude, you're going to have to go to school and find out

for yourself," Andy insists, finally breaking from his notebook. "Not to sound like *The Secret*, but you are the captain of your own destiny. If you decide you're not going to allow that accident scene to happen, then it's not going to happen."

"How do you know it won't?" I ask, exhausted.

"How do you know it will?" Andy answers. "You have free will, last I checked."

CHANGE 4-DAY 6

And, the jig is up.

When I "come home from school" on Friday with Andy, I drop my backpack on the kitchen table, grab a juice from the fridge, and head down the hall toward the TV room. Snoopy is jumping up on my knee, begging for a little attention. (In retrospect, he was probably trying to tell me something, like Lassie warning little Timmy of danger ahead.)

I call out for my mom while bending down to give Snoopy a cuddle, but she doesn't respond. She'd said she'd be home when I got back from school. "Dad?" I try. Andy follows sheepishly behind me. Which should've tipped me off . . .

When I turn the corner into the living room, there it is in all its mortifying glory: my Intervention. Like a scene from the reality TV show, only I haven't been shooting heroin. Or popping opiates. Or mainlining mouthwash. My crime was playing hooky from school for a week, trying to save the woman I love from myself.

No matter. Here is Mom, Dad, Tracy, Mr. Crowell, and Andy bringing up the rear, confronting me with my great big lie.

"I don't want you to feel threatened by this gathering," Tracy begins. "We are all here because we love you and are concerned about you."

Oh boy.

"Will you sit down?" Mom asks in her calmest therapist voice, gesturing to the empty lounger facing everybody in a semicircle.

"So what?" I start right in, defensive. "I didn't want to go to school."

"Why not?" Tracy inquires gently, tamping down the panic in her voice. She hates when things are out of order.

"I don't want to talk about it," I say, refusing to sit, and glancing over at Andy, who won't make eye contact with me for more than a second. Nor will Mr. Crowell. Hmmm, I wonder who ratted me out first. Maybe it was a one-two punch.

The veins in Dad's neck are about to break through the skin, Hulk-style. I'm disappointing him again, damaging his Changers Council brand. "Sit down," he orders in a tone that seems like I probably should. "You have to go to school. Legally, there's no choice in the matter, okay?"

Mom places a palm on his back. "And we need to talk about *why* you're not going to school."

"I said I don't want to talk about it."

"Is it something to do with this new V?" Dad asks, struggling to mask his annoyance. "Because from what I can see, this V is a home run. What complaints could you possibly have?"

"I don't have complaints, exactly."

"Well, what is it exactly, then?" Tracy presses.

I don't feel like partaking in a group therapy session. I lean back in the lounger, cross my (thick!) arms. I realize then that the posture feels like it looks imposing, a new color in my crayon box.

After an excruciating standoff, Tracy pulls out a piece of paper and places it on the table between us. "This is your schedule, you're all registered and ready to go."

"And I can get you caught up with the teachers," Mr. Crowell pipes in. "We will say that a parent fell ill and you had to stay home and take care of them."

"Fine," I say, as surly as possible.

"Listen. Turner has a truancy officer on call, and he's going to be trailing your butt to school on Monday morning," Dad says, bolting up. "So if you're not in first period homeroom with Mr. Crowell at 8:05 a.m., you will be reported, and trust me, you do not want to go down that road."

And with that, Dad walks out, his weak attempt at "understanding" done, I guess.

"I'll go to school," I say after several more moments of uncomfortable shifting in seats, everybody staring at me.

"I am really happy to hear that," Tracy says, "but of more import is exploring in this safe and supportive environment *why* you don't want to go in the first place."

"Sweetie, we want to help," Mom adds.

"Is there shame or guilt associated with this V?" Tracy prompts. "Because that's a perfectly acceptable reaction to a change as radical as this one."

"I'm not talking about this," I say flatly, glaring at Andy, hoping he was getting my telepathy message to ixnay on the Audrey-ay.

"Do you want me to leave?" he asks.

"No," I say. "I will. It's been fun, folks."

At that, I snatch up my schedule from the table, stomp

down the hall, and slam the door to my bedroom behind me—harder than I'd intended.

After a respectable twenty-minute break, Tracy knocks on my door, tentatively.

"Come in," I concede.

"I think I know what's up," she whispers, closing the door behind her. I kick out my desk chair for her, and she sits down, rolling it closer to me like she's about to let me in on a secret. Which she does.

Touchstones, it seems, are required by the Council to keep their own Chronicles, field notes, and observations about the Changers they are assigned to. Like Jane Goodall and her chimps.

Tracy had scanned back over her notes from freshman year when I was Drew, found where she'd recorded that I told her about the vision I'd had after kissing Audrey, and that it involved a guy named Kyle. Even then I was flipping out about how I was going to "save" Audrey from this animal when he inevitably threatened her life.

"I knew something was up on C4–D1," Tracy says quietly, "when I fobbed your Chronicling chip, and you grabbed my arm way too hard."

"I'm sorry," I say. "I wasn't aware."

Tracy unconsciously rubs her arm where I don't even remember grabbing her on Monday morning, right after I'd opened my Kyle packet and she was making sure I seared myself with the Changers emblem before leaving the house. I was so distraught finding out I was Kyle, hell-bent on destroying myself before crossing paths with Audrey at school, that I guess I wasn't paying attention to how I was acting. I didn't even feel it when I burned the emblem into my backside.

Tracy continues, "First things first, visions aren't always what they seem to be. Context is often missing, angles, etcetera. You're not some out-of-control maniac."

How would she know? I sure feel out of freaking control. I could be Lenny, accidentally squeezing the mouse to death with my dinner-plate hands.

"You can totally handle this V. It could even be an amazing, unexpected journey."

"Aren't they all," I snort.

"However you play it, you can't try and warn Audrey about something that may not even be the thing you imagine it is."

I roll my eyes; she catches it.

"Promise me you won't tell Audrey," she says. "You could be putting her in even more danger by telling her."

"How?"

"Your job is to focus on you," she answers, dodging the question. "Living your best life. Getting acquainted with your new V. It would be nice if Audrey could stay in your orbit as a friend, but she's been a liability for some time now, and deep down you know it. You can love her all you want. But you can't let that love imperil what we're all here to do. This is bigger than you."

"But how do I not talk to her?"

"Easy. You don't," Tracy snips. "We can reassign your homeroom—"

"NO!"

"Simplify things."

"No. I feel comfortable there, and, and . . . Mr. Crowell can keep tabs on us better if we're together. Just in case," I suggest, knowing Tracy is always onboard with additional monitoring.

"That makes sense," she says after mulling it over. "This new V is completely unknown to Audrey. All you have to do is keep it that way, resist the temptation to reignite the relationship. It'll naturally fade with Kim's disappearance. Just like the Cycle is designed to do. You need to lose your scooter. Maybe get a proper car? And I was thinking, why not try out for football again? Your Kyle dossier says you were MVP at your last high school."

"Yeah, maybe," I say, actually considering the prospect, since I would be able to maintain eyes on Jason and his Abider-leaning minions. Also, Audrey hates football, so me playing would keep her repelled and at a safe distance.

"It's going to be great, Kyle," Tracy urges, kinder now. "I have faith in you to do the right thing."

Heavy bullshit, even for her.

She points to my schedule, the Monday column: *Home-room, History, English, Math, French, College Prep, PE.* "All good?"

"Yeah," I say. "But can I ask you something?"

Tracy nods.

"Do kiss visions ever *not* happen at all?"

"Worry about tomorrow tomorrow," she says.

Which wasn't an answer. Only, it kind of was.

CHANGE 4-DAY 8

Audrey gazed at me over her shoulder from the front row of homeroom. Glanced away quickly, then looked right back, double-take style, like in cartoons. Eyes practically popping out of their sockets.

Ah-oooh-ga!

I shifted my weight from one leg to the other in the back of the class. As (per tradition) Mr. Crowell asked me to stand and introduce myself to my new (a.k.a. old) classmates. He shared with the class that I had recently relocated from Seattle, and that folks should introduce themselves to me, that I was a "real good guy."

Chloe whispered, loud enough for everybody to hear, "I'd climb that pole," and her crew offered up the requisite supporting snickers.

"Excuse me, Chloe?" Mr. Crowell said. "Was there something you'd like to ask Kyle?"

"Not here," she said, and winked real theatrically.

I smiled at Audrey the next time I caught her eye, but stopped myself halfway through. Her eyes darted away.

I didn't listen during the rest of homeroom, I was so totally fixated on figuring out a way to approach Audrey and confess that I'm Kim. But also that I'm Kyle, the dude who's going to be responsible for her death, *maybe*, per Tracy, if that little Mary Sunshine is to be believed.

How do I tell her the one part, without telling her the other?

I'm still going back and forth over the maddening conundrum of it all when I pop into the boys' bathroom in between homeroom and history. I barely register when two ninth grade guys part ways for me to pass to the urinal. How they stop talking and laughing when I get near.

When I come out of the bathroom, Audrey is waiting for me in the hallway, clutching her notebook to her chest.

"Hey, Kyle," she says. "My name's Audrey. Welcome to Central." She holds out her hand, the charm bracelet on full display. I pretend not to see it, though it is obvious she wants me to.

"Great to meet you," I say, taking her hand and feeling how small it is in mine. The bracelet tinkles when we shake.

"Do you need some help finding your first class?" Aud asks, peering at me with intensity, like she's a detective on the case. "It's a big school. Lot of new kids coming in."

"Uh . . . uh, sure."

"Let me see your schedule." She points at my backpack.

As we walk down the hallway, kids can't help but stare at me. It reminds me of my first day as Drew, except no one is eyeballing me like I'm their next meal. More like I'm Central's version of Captain America, at least a head taller than most everybody else, even some of the D-line from the football team, whom I recognize from when I played sophomore year.

"Well, this is it," Audrey chirps, lingering like she's waiting for me to say something.

"Okay, thanks. Really appreciate it."

"That all?" she says. It sounds like a dare.

"All?"

"All right. Everything all right?"

It takes every fiber of my will not to wink or nod or snatch her hand and run down the halls and out the front doors and drive far away where we can prepare to avoid our tragic future together.

"Yep," I say.

Audrey cringes. I don't blame her. *Yep* is the worst.

As she walks away, I realize she could break me. That I won't be able to avoid coming clean if I spend significant time in her presence.

My plan crystallizes in that instant: In order to keep my shizz together as long as I am Kyle, I need to get the hell out of dodge. Can't be that tough. I'll find a place to hunker down. Minimize contact, but keep tabs. After a year, I'll tell Audrey what happened, she'll understand, she always does. Then I'll choose any other Mono besides Kyle, so the car-crash scenario playing out becomes impossible. Changer life hack! Crisis averted!

"Dude, this is insane," Andy says as I stuff the last of my clothes into my trusty duffel and duck into the bathroom to pack up some toiletries.

"I don't know what else to do."

"You're really worrying me," Andy says, as I shove some toothpaste, a toothbrush, and deodorant into my bag, and try to zip the whole overstuffed thing.

"I've moved out before. To RaChas HQ."

"Which is presently an ash heap. Like your brain, apparently. You really think you can run away for a whole year?" he asks, chuckling. Which kind of makes me mad. "What are you going to do for money, shelter, food? You haven't thought this through. Trust me, I've been homeless and I've been housed, and housed is way better."

"You don't understand," I say, rummaging in my closet for a jacket. Dang, I forgot to buy something at ReRunz that'll fit my new frame. "Can I borrow your jacket?"

Without waiting for a reply, I grab Andy's oversized military coat from the back of the desk chair. As I do, he snatches it. And then we're each tugging on one end of the jacket like dogs over a chew toy.

"Dude, let go," he says.

"Don't be a douche. Let me take it, and I'll bring you another one when I come back."

I give one last yank on the jacket, and it comes free, sending Andy off-balance, stumbling in the space between us.

"You're the one being a douche," he says. "Totally selfish and self-centered, all in the supposed name of Audrey."

And then I sock him. Out of nowhere. My fist just reflexively cocked back, and I let it fly.

"What the . . . ?" he yelps, grabbing his eye and sitting back on my bed.

"I'm sorry," I say, shocked at myself.

"You're taking swings at me? This is crazy. You know that, right? I don't know if it's a hormonal imbalance, or maybe you're just an asshole now, but what the fuck, Kyle!"

"You wouldn't even have a place to stay if it weren't for me," I argue, trying to modulate my voice. "I risked everything to make that happen, so I have no clue where you get off telling me I'm the selfish one."

"Risked what, exactly? I already knew about Changers. Soon enough, everyone will. Secrets are never secrets forever. It's naïve that you people believe that."

"You people?" I yell, yanking the duffel and Andy's jacket off the floor. I hurl the jacket at him. "Keep it. It's too small anyway."

I storm out. He watches me for a few seconds, almost like he's seeing whether I'm actually going to leave. And then, as I'm stepping over the threshold, I hear his voice.

"If you walk out that door, I'm telling your parents," he says calmly. "Everything."

CHANGE 4-DAY 9

Obviously I couldn't leave.

Can't stay. Can't leave. Can't kill myself. Can't build an *Alien* sleeping capsule and seal the door for nine months.

So here I am, back at school, and Audrey is helpfully walking me to class after homeroom again, and this time she leans close, up on her tippy-toes, and says, "I feel like we've met before."

This is of course my cue to come out. It's like she intuits me, or thinks she does, and all I have to do is say it. Two little words: *It's me.* Even a nod or wink would suffice, and all would be well. At least in this moment.

But I can't do it.

So I take the fraidy-cat route and ask, "Sorry, what was that?"

It's obvious I heard what she said. She seems humiliated, regroups: "I asked if you wanted to sit together at lunch today."

"Yep," I say. "Catch you later." It's official: I'm the *yep* guy. Maybe that alone will put her off.

In American civilization, the teacher starts lecturing about the Baron de Montesquieu and the ambition of man. Separation of governmental powers into executive, legislative, and judicial branches. Which I guess was pretty forward-thinking for the middle of the eighteenth century. And yet this guy who wrote all about liberty and how government should be set up so no man should be afraid of another man wasn't in support of American independence? Convenient inconsistencies. Akin to *The Changers Bible*.

The teacher segues into the theory of environmental determinism, how some people believe where we live makes us who we are. Hitler was into that BS, used it as proof that white Nordic cultures were superior to others. And Thomas Jefferson used it to rationalize African colonization, because tropical climates supposedly make people who live in them "lazy," "promiscuous," and "uncivilized." Whereas people from northern climates are "hard-working," "rational," and thus completely "civilized." Gross. I wonder how the climate explains Jefferson fathering six kids with his slave Sally Hemings?

The theory seems so stupid now, insidious even. But people still believe equally dangerous things, about who should be allowed to marry, or pee in a public bathroom, or not have children, or have sex with each other, or serve in the military, or live in safety. And these days, they aren't even bothering with the fancy dressing of a phony science excuse. Change may be coming, but it isn't coming fast enough. Look at the Abiders. The more difference is sewn into the fabric of humanity, the more a certain segment is going to feel threatened and try to extinguish it. Makes me want to bail on this whole Changers mission and live a tiny life in isolation. Me and Audrey in a cottage, in a seaside village with a post office and a coffee shop. Maybe a used bookstore. No responsibility to change anybody's mind, ever. About anything.

* * *

Over lunch I keep it to small talk with Audrey. She's still wearing the charm bracelet, letting it creep out of her shirt cuff as she moves her arms to speak or eat. She keeps asking searching questions, and I volley every single one back in a way that proves I'm a newbie here at Central, fresh off the boat from the Pacific Northwest, moving here because my mother got a professorship at Vanderbilt, like the packet from the Changers Council instructed. It's scary how easy it can be to lie once you get going.

As lunch progresses, and it becomes clearer Kim is not going to join the party, I can tell Aud is losing heart. Which breaks mine. Afterward we walk toward the one class we have together: environmental science. On the way, I notice Kris taping something to the lockers at the end of the hall. When we get closer, I see what it is: a stack of purple flyers with Kim's face on them. Underneath: *Have you seen me?*

"Any luck?" Audrey asks Kris, while I barely manage to stand by, my face flushing hot and purple as those flyers, I'm sure.

"Nothing," Kris mumbles, sticking the last piece of tape to the bottom of another flyer, near a number to call with any information about the disappearance of Kim Cruz. "The police still won't treat it as a missing persons case."

Audrey leans into Kris, and then they embrace for a long time, while I continue to panic inside.

"Kris, this is Kyle. Kyle, Kris," Audrey says.

I reach out my hand to shake Kris's, and he turns away.

"Nice to meet you," I say.

"Is it?" Kris asks.

"Sorry," Audrey interrupts. "We both lost somebody we care deeply about."

"That's terrible," I say.

"You wouldn't understand," Kris snots back, his face red, like he's been crying.

"Well, I'm really sorry about your friend," I say, and I can tell Audrey's eyes are boring into mine from the side, searching for ANY clue that I recognize who or what Kim Cruz is. I go on: "I once lost somebody close to me, and it was the hardest thing imaginable."

Which is true. Chase. Nana. Audrey. Myself.

Kris mumbles a reluctant, "Thanks," and wipes his nose with the back of his hand.

"If there's anything I can do—"

"Can you bring my friend back?" he snaps.

Yeah, in fact, I can.

"Come on," Audrey whispers, and squeezes Kris on the shoulder as we pass by.

I wonder how Aud must be dealing with seeing Kim's face all milk-cartoned around, knowing full well that Kim ain't exactly "missing," and she sure as heck ain't ever coming back.

Tracy and Destiny were right. I'd made her complicit in my deceptions. I'd put Audrey in a position where she had to lie to someone she cared for too. All to protect someone who was presently dicking her over.

The day ends in PE. We're running a mini, modified parkour course, and the teacher disappears for a minute, then returns with Coach Tyler. They're both staring at me from across the gym. Pointing.

Moi? I gesture. Coach Tyler waves me over. I run up to him, like old times on the football field when I was Oryon.

"Where'd you play ball before?"

"Someplace," I start, trying to remember the dossier.

"Speak up, son."

"Seattle. Northeastern High." *(I think.)*

"What position?"

"QB."

"Why aren't you playing here?" Coach demands, while the PE teacher returns to the rest of class.

"I don't know," I reply. "There's a lot going on, with the move."

"Yeah, I heard about some family matters, from Mr. Crowell. I'm sorry to hear about your father's illness."

"Thank you, sir," I say, falling right back in line.

"Is his health improved?"

"Yessss," I respond, anxious about where this is headed.

"Good. I want you to play for us, then. We start ten minutes after the final bell. Today. I'll leave some practice gear in the locker room for you."

And BAM, I'm on the football team, taking snaps at practice after school and being given pointers by—of all people—Jason, who takes a special interest in me, because, as he says, "Something about you reminds me of me."

Shudder.

The new QB-1 this year, Darryl, who had been in Jason's shadow for the past three seasons, apparently sucked at last week's game. Central got spanked by thirty-one points, with Darryl throwing five interceptions on the night, before (mercifully) spraining his thumb. The second I throw my first twenty-yard spiral and hit the receiver smack in the middle of his numbers at practice, it is clear there's going to be a new QB-1 in town.

I have to say, there was something supernatural about how my body moved on the field. It was like the pads were sewn to my muscles, the helmet an extension of my skull, nothing like when Oryon was bouncing like a bobble-head doll all over the field in the same equipment. As Kyle, the harder I ran, the more I wanted to run. The more snaps I took, the more accurate my passes. It was like I didn't even have to think; the ball went where I wanted whenever I released it. I had no idea where the skill was coming from, but it wasn't the worst to have dominion over my body in a way I'd never had, not even as Ethan.

Coach Tyler and Jason kept eyeballing each other like, *This boy's a ringer.* In fact, I think the offensive coach might've uttered that exact phrase, right before he told me to get some rest and come back tomorrow, that my new jersey number (8, Jason's old number) was going to be waiting for me, and that my first game was Friday.

CHANGE 4-DAY 11

Audrey and I are in a routine. We walk together from homeroom to first period, then wave to one another at lunch, and then I avoid her for the rest of the day. I eat alone, but I catch her checking me out at least a few times during lunch period. Nobody sits with me, so I gobble my meal as quickly as possible with my headphones on, head down.

"Howdy," this guy Brady says to me in the locker room while we're suiting up for practice. I recognize him from English class last year. He maybe said two words to me (well, Kim), but I didn't get a vibe one way or the other from him. Good or evil.

"Excuse me?" I say.

"I'm Brady." He holds out a fist.

"Kyle," I say, tapping his knuckles with mine, then go back to tying my shoulder pads.

"I know who you are. Everybody knows who you are."

"Really?"

"Really," he says. "I heard Coach yesterday, already talking about a D-1 scholarship. And my sister, she's a sophomore. She says there's a running bet for whoever goes up and talks to you first in the cafeteria and gets invited to sit down. I think it's up to fifty bucks.

"That can't be true."

"Lotta rumors about you too," Brady continues, even though I'm not trying to keep this convo going.

I guess I'm curious about what these "rumors" are, but there is no way I'm letting him think I care. I nod, tie my cleats.

"Chloe, you met her? Head cheerleader? Kind of hot? Anyway, she says you used to be a model for Louis Vuitton. She says there's a picture of you shirtless in one of her European magazines."

I laugh.

"It's true!" he says. "It is, isn't it?"

I say nothing, grab my helmet, and jog out to the field.

The coaches are all over me, trying to get me caught up on memorizing the plays, how to run our offense. It's a lot to remember, and to be honest, they sort of treat me like I'm dumb. Well, who can blame them—they've been coaching Jason as QB-1 for the last three years.

Speaking of whom, as practice is letting out, Jason gets all up in my business, hopping around and quizzing me on plays, imparting little tips about our crosstown rival's defense. I see Audrey walking up in the distance behind him, can't take my eyes off her. And of course Jason notices. *Great.*

"What time are we leaving?" Audrey asks him, though she's peering at me through my face mask. I kind of pull a lips-closed grin, but I don't think she can see my mouth.

"Give me a few minutes," he says, like she's a pesky mosquito. "This is an important game tomorrow night."

"No problem," I say, "I have to get home anyway."

"You need a ride?" Jason offers eagerly.

"I'm good."

"Audrey, this here is my protégé, Kyle."

"We've met."

"Oh, you have?" he asks suggestively.

Uh oh, here comes the boom . . .

"Homeroom," I quickly add, but it sounds muffled through my helmet.

Jason stands quiet for a few seconds, head swiveling back and forth, back and forth. I'm wondering which way this is going to go, but after a beat, he slaps my ass real hard, and nods Audrey off, "We'll be done in five, meet you at the car."

She starts walking away, and I watch her go. Jason watches me watch her.

"Focus!" he blurts menacingly, right up in my face, then slaps my helmet on both sides with his palms. He starts cracking himself up like a lunatic. "She *likes* you."

"I don't even know her, man."

"Well, she wants to know you. We we were worried that she was into chicks, but I bet if anybody could turn her, you could."

There really is no bottom with this guy.

"I'm sure your sister is dope, but I'm not up for a relationship," I say.

"You a fag or something?" For a second I'm terrified, the memories of all the evil Jason has done to me, to my friends, rushing back. I feel sweat rolling down my spine, adrenaline spiking. Inside, I'm still Drew, Oryon, Kim. My fight-or-flight hasn't calibrated to my new hulking form. Then Jason chuckles, low and greasy like. "Just kidding, brah. No fag throws a football like you do. Am I right?"

CHANGE 4-DAY 12

We won the game 38–3. I threw for three touchdowns. Ran for two more.

At the final whistle, my teammates all rushed me one after the other, ramming into me in midair. It took me about four times of almost being toppled over before realizing I was supposed to jump up too, to slam our bodies together in the air. Endless slapping my helmet. Pure glee and optimism on everybody's sweaty faces. The coaches beaming, like their jobs are secured for another year and they can pay for their daughters' braces. Coach Tyler gave me the game ball, and he never gives out game balls.

When I finally got a break and took off my helmet, a cyclone of maroon, black, and white charged at me, a trio of Central cheerleaders, with one launching herself onto my body, wrapping her legs tight around my waist, and *squeezing*. When she pulled back and I got a full glimpse of her face, I realized it was, of course, Chloe. As I tried to peel her off me, I caught Audrey's eye up in the stands. She sort of waved, and I tried to free an arm to wave back.

Next thing I knew, a light flared on, blinding me, and a microphone was shoved in my face: a local TV news reporter asking me about the forty-two-yard pass into the end zone in the first quarter. I don't even know what I said, "Blah blah blah, instinct, blah blah blah, couldn't do it without my teammates," but afterward Jason told me to expect my phone to be ringing with recruiters starting first thing Monday morning. (That's what happened to him, after all.)

I'd been Kyle less than two weeks, played a single game, and I was already a local hero, a school savior, a model in Europe, the subject of a sex raffle.

I was already everything to everyone, and I'd done next to nothing to deserve it. It was such a sharp turn from Kim, Oryon, Drew. So plainly unfair. It made my stomach hurt.

But also. If I'm honest. It felt a little bit awesome too.

CHANGE 4-DAY 19

We won again. At home. This time a shutout, 28–0. I threw three of the four touchdowns we scored. Everybody was saying there were more fans in the stands than usual. People already speculating about a state championship run.

I know it's stupid football, and I could take it or leave most of it, really. All the pomp of the march through the crowd and out to the field, kids idolizing you like you're a god, strange adults holding signs with your name and number on them, proud of you for being able to throw a piece of leather successfully to another person who's good at catching it. That can all go. But the game itself, the math and mystery when I'm running a play, it's practically the only time I'm not worrying about Audrey. Or my vision of her death. I'm only fixating on where to put that ball.

When the game ended, the team and what seemed like half the student body hit up a kegger at one of the guys' houses. The usual parents-out-of-town, spoiled-rich-kid-with-lawn-furniture-ending-up-in-the-pool deal. Andy came too, excited to be reaping the benefits of rolling with the star quarterback, everybody sidling up to him to get information about the mysterious Kyle Smith.

For kicks, whenever someone asks something, Andy confirms it, whispering as though the receiver of the infor-

mation is the chosen one being let in on Kyle's little secrets.

Model in Paris? Yes, for a year while taking a break from high school.

Auditioning for the next big teen TV series? Totally.

Crown prince of a small but powerful, wealthy foreign nation? Yes, but please don't tell anybody; he must lay low for security reasons.

"That girl wants to make out with me," Andy whispers, pointing across the TV room at Chloe's minion, Brit.

"Trust me, you don't want any part of that," I say.

The front door of the house suddenly blows open, and it's . . . Jason. The guy who never stops hanging around high school parties. He's flanked by two friends of the exact same type and disposition, from the football team five years before. And they have hard liquor. A ton of it.

"Really? Him?" Andy seethes. "Isn't he like forty?"

"You better make yourself scarce unless you want round two with your archnemesis," I say, getting my phone out to call Andy a Lyft.

He scoots out as Jason shouts, "My nizzle!"

Jason practically sprints over to man-hug me, making a big show of it in front of everybody in the room. He's already drunk. Or high. Or both.

"What's up?" I manage, as I see Audrey slip in the door behind him.

"You kicked some ass tonight!"

"Thanks," I say.

"We are going to rule the school this season," he slurs, then leans in and whispers, "I have a surprise for you later."

My ear is damp from his booze breath. It's hard not to

recoil, but I have to keep my enemies close, especially now. He goes over to crank up the sound system, then sing/yells at the top of his register: "*It's getting hot in here, so take off all your clothes!*" as three sophomore girls surround him and start undulating together like some sort of twenty-first-century Roman orgy.

I feel like leaving, but then Audrey approaches and chirps super brightly, "Hi, Kyle."

"Hey," I say, taken a bit off guard.

"Not exactly Alvin Ailey," she says, jerking a thumb toward her brother's display.

"Oh, well," I stammer, flustered at her being so close.

"Great game tonight."

"I thought you hated football," I slip.

"Says who?" Audrey asks, narrowing her eyes.

"Your brother said something, like that you think it's for meatheads or—"

"Oh," she giggles nervously. Come to think of it, she always seems nervous around me now. "Well?"

"Well what?" I ask.

"Are you a meathead?" Audrey lifts her shoulders an inch, drops her chin. Is she . . . flirting?

"Sometimes." I lift my shoulders too, like we're mirror reflections of each other.

"Good to know," Audrey says cheekily.

We both fall silent, glance around the room. I wonder if she can hear my breathing, because it's deafening to me. This whole scene reminding me of the first post–football game party we went to together freshman year, when we were cheerleaders. How naïve and young we were, so excited to be around all the cool kids, even though they were anything but. How we picked our way through the bacchanalia trying to find a quiet spot—until we came across Jason snapping photos of a girl who had passed out, her underwear exposed.

God, he's a creep.

I turn to Audrey, my desire to confess reinflamed by my trip down memory lane. She swivels to face me. We stand like that, like we're at the altar, the words so close on my tongue. *I'm Kim. I'm all of them. I'm yours.*

"What is it?" she asks, sensing something.

"I was thinking about how sexist this song is," I blurt. "*I got a friend with a pole in the basement?*"

"Yeah, it is sexist, but it's got nothing on *I'll let you lick the lollipop,*" Audrey says, cocking her head at me, like tectonic plates are shifting in her brain. We go back to awkwardly surveying the happenings in the room around us.

"I gotta say, Kyle, that was some pretty lady-friendly analysis for a meathead," Audrey finally says, breaking the silence. And then, "These parties always suck."

You can say that again.

And then, as she pivots around, Audrey brushes her side against mine. Not sexually, more playful, warm, like a cat on the leg of a sofa.

Oh man.

As much of a half-wit as he is, Jason knew it: Audrey does like me. Like, *likes me* likes me. WTF does that mean?

On the one hand, it feels amazing and right and exactly what should be happening—her drawn to me because of some sort of essential me-ness. We're soul mates! Pulled toward each other in the inexplicable way poets have written about through the ages.

On the other hand, what if she's only digging on me *because* of my outside, falling prey to the external like everybody else? Never mind that Audrey seems to have gotten over her pining for Kim super freaking fast. Yes, it's twisted, this messed-up part of me that's jealous. Jealous of MYSELF! But if Audrey has given up and moved on to the next shiny object, how strong was that connection to begin with?

At least she's wearing the bracelet. Which means she's still searching for me . . . right? I could tell her. I *should* tell her.

But I can't. So I say, "Yep," and excuse myself.

And then I start drinking.

Five Jägermeister shots later, I suddenly care less about A, B, C, D, and all of the above. I brush off Audrey, keeping a safe distance and making it easy by falling into gross fratbrah behavior with Jason and his buddies, who keep passing me shooter after shooter, with watery beer chasers. Kids keep coming up to me like they're paying tribute to the king, like I'm Kanye in my leather semicircle VIP booth at the club, and they all come to fist-bump me over the draped red-velvet rope. Everyone trying to connect with me somehow, so many exaggerated smiles and, "Yo, man, this! Yo, man, that!" The immediate blind worship so far removed from any of my prior experiences it makes me feel like the bug man in the *Men in Black* skin suit. If only all of them could see what I look like underneath.

Jason sidles up to me with two Solo cups of beer in his

hands and whispers, "You want your surprise now?"

He slings an arm around me, the beer sloshing out of the cup and onto the back of my neck and shirt, which first I'm annoyed at, but then almost as quickly I don't care, because my gums feel numb, and I'm dizzy, and I'm an imposter, and nothing matters. Jason leads me up some stairs and then down a hall, through a bedroom door.

Inside, there are two girls in front of a chest of drawers, studying themselves in the mirror. They spin around when they see our reflections behind them.

"What's going on?" I mumble, so very drunk.

"It's your MVP trophy for winning tonight," Jason says, pulling the door closed.

The girls giggle, press themselves together, and Jason hands them each a cup filled with beer. They both take big gulps. And then another. They seem so young. Like Drew was.

"Drink up," Jason encourages, roaching up on the girl to the right. He puts a meaty hand on her cheek, yanks it sideways for a sloppy kiss, juts his chin toward me. On cue, the girl on the left takes another swig, leaves her beer on the dresser, then slinks over to me, stretching to kiss me full on, open-mouth. I can't really not kiss back.

It is at this point that my addled brain realizes that by *trophy* Jason meant a living, breathing human being. He kills the lights, and the girl with me begins making out even more forcefully. I don't know where Jason and the other girl went, or what they're doing, only that this girl is pushing me backward toward the fluffy bed, her hands traveling down to my belt. She starts undoing the buckle, and I grab her to make her stop, scoot back.

"You sure you want to do this?" I ask. "What's your name?" As I talk, I realize I can barely understand myself. I feel like my brain is in a pickle jar.

"Jenny," she answers, climbing on top of me, quickly undressing. My head is spinning.

"Are you okay with this?" I ask, and she murmurs something that sounds like yes. Then she mumbles something else before her head goes limp and she collapses on the bed.

"Jenny?" I whisper. "Jenny, are you okay?"

But there's no answer.

She's not moving. I shake her gently.

Nothing.

"Jenny?" I try louder.

"Dude, what are you doing?" I hear from somewhere in the room, but I can't tell where. Maybe the floor? It's Jason's voice. "She wants you."

I stand up, the room is all off-kilter, I have to force myself not to vomit.

"What'd you put in those drinks?" I say, but I'm not sure it's coming out like I intend.

I can see Jason on the other side of the room. He's on top of the other girl, and they're on a blanket. She's in the same state as Jenny.

"Something's wrong. They need help," I say, but my words jumble again.

"Are you crazy?" he hisses. "Be cool, man."

I lean back over Jenny, put my ear close to her nose, and feel a few solid breaths. She's alive. Thank god. I cover her up, reach in my pocket for my phone to call 911.

"What are you doing?" Jason says, sounding angry.

"Calling an ambulance."

"What the fuck for?"

The door cracks open: "Jason, I need the keys, can you get—"

It's Audrey.

Now she's stopped midsentence, jaw frozen open, spotting me by the bed, Jenny passed out under the blankets. Audrey flees the room before I can say or do anything. I drop my phone.

"Goddammit!" Jason yells, and he pulls the blanket around his waist and hustles down the hallway after her. "This is your fault!"

He isn't wrong, I think. Then my vision goes dark.

My mind fights to keep me awake. I have to report him to the police.

Should I report him to the police?

If I report him, I'm implicating myself.

But maybe I *should* be implicated.

I didn't know. How could I know he'd dose those girls. Dose me too?

But I should've realized. Because I know Jason.

Time spins, colors bleeding together. *Breathe.*

I get up, splash water on my face, make myself throw up in the toilet, just as Jason returns, weaving back into the bedroom wrapped in nothing but a tasseled chenille blanket, saying he couldn't find Audrey. He doesn't seem to care.

He pokes a toe at the girl comatose on the floor.

"April," he trills, shoving her harder with his foot. "Aaaapril."

She doesn't move. Jason just laughs, drunk and high (on god knows what).

"Where's Audrey?"

"Who gives a shit?" he snorts. "Such a nosy little bitch." He scratches under his arm, smells his fingers.

"And these girls?"

"Just some freshmen ass," he says.

"So you, what? Doped them?"

"Dude, they wanted this. It's just sex. You're the QB! You get some. They get bragging rights. It's a win-win."

"But if they're freshmen, you banging April is illegal." (Same for the roofies Jason must have slipped in their beer.) "You're nineteen. She could be fourteen. That's statutory rape."

At this, Jason's face goes pale, no doubt less concerned with the moral failing of drugging girls to have sex with them than losing any chance at a football scholarship once his knee heals.

"Dude, being accused of that fake shit is every man's nightmare," he sputters.

"You should probably split," I say, thinking of nothing so much as Chase, and how when he saw Jason assaulting me as Drew freshman year, he didn't make polite conversation but instead beat Jason's face into tapioca. I wonder why I'm not doing the same. Because I certainly could.

As Jason yanks on his clothes, I ask, trying to sound casual, "How much did you give them?"

"Look who's curious now," he says. "Not much, half a pill each. Just trying to give us a little fun, man."

And then he leaves the room, with just me and the

passed-out girls in it, and disappears into the thumping party below.

Soon as Jason's gone, I check on April to make sure she's still breathing too. She is. I get out my phone, google how long roofies take to wear off, if I can do anything to speed up the process. I'm woozy and my muscles feel like bungee cords, but at least I'm conscious. I'm pretty sure Jason slipped me Ecstasy, since it seemed like what he was on. I remember hearing him talking in the locker room when I was Oryon about how X makes sex so much better.

I notice April is naked from the waist up. Luckily I have two years of experience with bras. I wiggle hers on, prop her head to the side on a pillow (in case she pukes), then head over to Jenny on the bed—when I notice the door cracking open again.

"Hello," I call out, "can somebody help me?"

It's Audrey. Another expression of sheer horror on her face. With the lights on, this scene probably appears way worse than it did when she burst in before.

"Can you help me finish getting clothes on them?" I ask, struggling.

Audrey is reluctant, but pads over silently, and I hold the sheet up so as to give Jenny her privacy while Audrey slips her arms through her shirt, not that Jenny was noticing.

"It's a little late for that, don't you think?" Audrey says. "Here, lift her chin."

We finish dressing Jenny in silence, then I pull up the blankets, prop her ear to pillow in case she vomits too.

Then we wait. Audrey across the room on a window seat, me on the bed next to Jenny, checking her breathing every couple of minutes. It seems like Audrey might have a lot to say, but she's not saying it.

I scroll through my phone again, feverishly researching party drugs, and after a few more minutes I offer, "From what I can tell, it could be three or four hours until this wears off. You should go home, I'll deal from here."

"I'll stay," she says. She goes over to where April's and Jenny's purses are on the dresser, fishes through for their wallets in hopes of finding IDs. April has a card with her address, but Jenny doesn't. She opens Jenny's phone, but can't get past the security code.

"It seems like you have some experience with stuff like this," I say.

"All high school girls have experience with stuff like this," she replies flatly.

"Listen," I start, but stop when I catch Audrey's expression. It's fallen. Confused. Worse: disappointed. So disappointed, for the first time I'm actually relieved she doesn't know it's me underneath the Kyle muscle suit.

We sit in silence for a few more minutes. Unsure what else to do, I go back to scrolling through my phone to read more about roofies. One blog says they're supposed to make you "lose your inhibitions," feel more "affectionate," have more "sexual interest," when you're on them. Did a dude write this crap? Passing out cold is not "sexual interest."

I'm such an idiot, I didn't notice anything was wrong with Jenny until it was too late.

"I know you didn't drug them," Audrey says out of nowhere.

"Oh, thank god," I say. "I swear, I had no idea he was going to—"

"I know," she cuts me off. She seems sad.

"Do you want to sit on the bed?" I ask, before realizing how it sounds. "I mean, get some rest until they wake up?"

"I'm good."

"I'm sorry this is happening," I say.

"It doesn't sound like it's really your fault."

"I should've guessed something was up."

"Why would you? You're just a guy."

I'm kissing somebody, deeply, the softest lips I've ever felt. I reach my hand around both sides of her warm cheeks, kiss more intensely for a few seconds before pulling back, slowly opening my eyes and realizing I'm kissing . . .

"Kyle. Kyle. KYLE!"

Whoa, what? Wait. I jolt awake, Audrey jabbing my shoulder to rouse me. I squint, disoriented. Finally I realize where I am. In the upstairs bedroom where the horrible scene played out.

"Good morning, morning glory," Audrey says sarcastically.

I stand up, notice Jenny and April groggily gathering themselves, not entirely sure what happened. (Thankfully nothing close to what could have.) Sunlight peeks through the curtains, a few early birds *cheep-cheeping* outside in the trees.

"Hey, aren't you the quarterback?" Jenny says.

I nod.

"Did we?"

"We did not," I assure her.

She seems relieved.

The four of us head downstairs. There are kids sleeping

all over the living room. Draped across every surface like those melting clocks in Dalí paintings. We have to hold onto the railing to step over one of my offensive linemen, Buster, who's sprawled across the last four stairs, a half-empty bottle of malt liquor clasped in his hand. I see his car keys dangling from his wallet chain. I pluck them free, figure he won't be needing them anytime soon.

We go outside, the humid air thick, making the hair on my arms instantly damp. I click the fob until I hear a car unlock, then I help April and Jenny into the backseat of Buster's 4x4, open the door for Audrey to ride shotgun, and back down the driveway, avoiding as many empty bottles as I can.

It's silent in the car on the way to April's house, except for directions Siri announces from the phone. The wind whips through the open windows, blowing stray Popeyes napkins around the wheel well. In the rearview I see Jenny scrolling through her Snapchat, watching silly five-second videos from the night before. Shared memories that last as long as a sneeze, then vanish as if they never happened at all.

CHANGE 4-DAY 21

Today, while we (ostensibly) did some homework, I told Andy almost everything about what happened at the party. When I finished, he said I should report Jason to the local police for drugging and sexually assaulting a minor.

I dialed the station three times, hanging up each time before anyone answered. What was I going to say? I wasn't exactly the perfect witness.

Audrey tried to explain to April and Jenny more about what had happened as she walked them to the door when we dropped them home. (Well, what *almost* happened in my case with Jenny, and who knows what happened with Jason and April before he took off.) Audrey gave them her phone number and said for them to call if they had any questions, or wanted to talk, or wanted to report that they were dosed by Jason. She said she would back them up, and that I would too.

Both girls half-listened, anxious to get inside, take a shower, sleep it off, and move on. It was hard for them to see the upside of bringing charges against the former QB, of stirring up a whole hornet's nest of accusations that would expose them to the worst kind of trolling. And for what? It wasn't like Jason would ever do time. And they'd be seen as pariahs. We'd all read enough news stories. We'd all seen the *Hunting Ground* documentary.

When Audrey came back to the borrowed car and got in, her face was flushed. I asked her if she was okay.

"Sure," she said, and nothing else all the way back to the party house to return Buster's truck.

I parked, then killed the engine, trying one last time before Audrey could hop out. "I'm here if you want to talk about anything," I said.

She shot me a glare of pure disdain. "What could you possibly know about feeling powerless?"

CHANGE 4-DAY 22

I need to talk to somebody, but there's nobody who will truly understand. Nobody I can trust. Tracy? Hell no. Mr. Crowell? Yes, definitely, back in the day, but now I'd be too afraid he'd rat me out to Tracy, who would in turn rat me out to Turner and the Council. And then my father would find out. And Dad is obviously not an option. He couldn't handle even the *idea* of my sexual assault when I was Drew. I can only imagine the wave of disappointment he'd drown me in if I confessed I was almost the perpetrator, because I was wasted, and had hurt feelings, and wasn't clued into the fact that my date had been drugged into oblivion. He sees Kyle as the answer to his every Changer prayer. I've heard him bragging to all his Council friends about how great it's going to be to have Kyle representing Changer Nation.

I wish I could talk to Mom. But after all the trouble I gave her last year, with running away, living with the Ra-Chas, being so constantly and deeply depressed—I can't make her live with the knowledge of what her son allowed to happen.

This afternoon during study hall, I even paced back and forth in front of the school counselor Ms. Hayes's office, contemplating going in, but I didn't have the guts to knock on the door. I also bailed on football practice, not telling anybody in advance, a cardinal sin in Coach Tyler's book. I couldn't bear to see Jason's dumb face, was afraid of what I might do to it when I did.

I also avoided Audrey. Purposely came late to homeroom, left early to use the bathroom, studiously avoided her in the halls and at lunch, skipping our shared class. It wasn't until I was leaving for home that I finally saw her, exiting the counselor's office that I'd been too punk to go in.

"Hey," she said from behind me.

"Oh, hi," I responded, pretending I hadn't noticed her.

Audrey picked up her backpack that was sitting on a bench. "Do you want to get some coffee with me? I have my mom's car, I can give you a ride."

The cute twentysomething barista pours a foam heart on my latte. Right in front of Audrey. The flirtation is thick.

"I think this is for you," Audrey says sheepishly, passing me the coffee with the barista's number inked on the sleeve.

We sit at a rear table and sink into the couch beside one another. But not too close.

"Does that happen often?" Audrey asks, almost sort of wounded. It reminds me of how people treated Destiny while I stood by feeling like an invisible sack of trash in the corner. (*Be careful what you wish for* the obvious takeaway there.)

"No, not too often," I finally answer. And it's not a lie, given I've only lived twenty-two days of it. "It's just people being people."

"Easy for you to say."

"I'm sure guys give you their numbers all the time. Or girls. Whatever . . ." I trail off.

And POOF.

It slipped out. I didn't mean to let it. I recall the kiss vision. The crash. I've got to stop this familiar train. She can't know I know her. *Know her* know her. You know?

"You're not a bad guy, Kyle," she says then. "I know you think that Friday night was about you, but it wasn't."

"It kind of was."

She edges closer, puts a warm hand on my knee. Which sends an electric current through all my limbs, and ends with a whoosh through my heart. "Everyone makes mistakes. Trust me, I have made plenty."

I resist asking what she means by that.

"I talked with Ms. Hayes confidentially about all of it," Audrey continues. "April and Jenny want to pretend like it didn't happen. I don't even think they believe it happened. It's always like this."

"He's done this before?" I ask, aware of the answer.

"Last year he tried it on Chloe, the head cheerleader. But my friend Kim knocked the drink out of her hand and called him out." She checks my expression, maybe fishing for any recognition of the incident in question.

I play dumb. "Kim sounds badass."

"Yeah. She is. Was. Is," Audrey cycles quickly.

"That has to be hard for you. He's still your family."

"Family is what you make it," she says, sounding like every queer self-help book I've ever read. "My brother needs to be held accountable for what he does. But he never is."

"He will be, one day," I say, but I'm not so sure.

"On Earth Two, maybe," Audrey quips.

It feels so warm and familiar between us.

"Well, I should probably get going," I say, every cell in my body telling me not to.

"Yeah, me too."

But it's obvious she doesn't want to leave either.

CHANGE 4-DAY 27

We won the game again. Woo. But it was by a lesser margin. I simply wasn't feeling it. Barely tried. Yet still managed to throw two touchdowns, and the running backs did the rest.

Honestly, I kind of want to quit football. (Like I did as Oryon.) The exaltation of playing, of capitalizing on what my body was built to do, can't outweigh how gutting it feels to spend time with Jason—the dog crap you can never get out of your shoe tread, even with a toothpick. We never said a word to each other about what happened at the party. Or him being a serial sexual predator, because 1) in his mind he isn't, and 2) me confronting him would blow up my life even more. I mean, why would it be my duty to punish Jason? I tried that in the past. Nothing changed.

The definition of insanity is repeating the same behavior and expecting different results. I read that somewhere.

Anyway, the point being, nothing I say to Jason is going to make him have a come-to-Jesus moment where he says, *My, I have been a garbage person my whole life, haven't I? I'm heading to therapy STAT!* I'm not fixing that dude. I can't even fix myself. And my energy is better spent elsewhere, keeping my Audrey vision from coming true.

Which is why I decided to say "peace out" to the

Changers Mixer, so I could avoid hearing again about my responsibility to #maketheworldabetterplace.

I told Mom I had the runs. Doused hot water on my face, pushed it into my hair to look like sweat, and opened the door to the bathroom to let my concerned mom in, Dad right on her heels. "He feels clammy," Mom said, touching her cheek to the back of my neck.

Dad was furious. "The mixers are required." This was not acceptable perfect-model-Kyle behavior.

Mom shot him a look. The kind that said, *Uh-unh, not again, buddy.* As in, *You messed with my kid last year, and that almost tore us all apart, but I'm not letting you do it again, because if you do, that's going to be it.* (At least that's how I interpreted her look.)

"It's one meeting," she said sternly. "He's attended every other one."

"Come on, he played four quarters last night and he was fine," Dad argued.

"Well, he's NOT fine now. What's he going to learn this year that he hasn't learned the last three? What's he going to miss, a potato-sack race? A dunk tank? A pie-eating contest?" Mom asked, making the mixer sound corny AF. "I mean if he's contagious, he probably shouldn't be around other people anyway!"

Dad studied me, the fake perspiration on my head, thought about it for a few seconds, and then gave in, sucking his teeth. "I'll get you caught up on what you missed when I get home."

I grunted (because I was too sick to talk).

The mixers are supposed to feel like reunions, but never

actually do, because everybody's new in their V's, and nobody can tell who's who, and plus, we aren't really friends anyway seeing as we all go to different schools, and have nothing in common besides being Changers who happen to be dispersed throughout the Southeast. It's like expecting everyone to be friends because they all live in Tampa or like avocado rolls.

Mom helped me into bed and brought me some orange Gatorade with ice, which has always been my favorite thing when I'm under the weather. As we heard Dad close the garage and take off, Mom confided, "I'm so happy I don't have to go to that mixer either," and winked.

Which made it seem like she might be onto me but doesn't care. With Andy still at work and Mom exiting to "reclaim her time," I flipped open my laptop and started binge-watching *Battlestar Galactica* from the beginning.

What is it about witnessing the end of life as we know it that makes you feel so much better?

CHANGE 4-DAY 28

Tracy came over first thing this morning, after missing me at the mixer yesterday. Making sure I wasn't still "sickly," and couldn't "infect the baby," she perched a hip on the bed, her growing belly cloaked in a cornflower-blue linen tunic, and grilled me on my life as Kyle thus far.

Turner the Lives Coach apparently sits down with each Y-4 Changer at their final mixer, to get a preliminary vibe about how our Cycles are wrapping up, now that we've had the opportunity to experience at least a taste of all our lives.

"I'll need you to write him an e-mail with an update for your file," Tracy says. "And there's another matter."

I sit up in bed.

"There's a second Changer at Central," she reveals matter-of-factly.

"Really? Who?" I ask.

"Her name's Charlie, and she's a freshman."

"Charlie?"

"Yes, Charlene, goes by Charlie," Tracy clarifies.

I was actually surprised. I always wondered whether there was another Changer at Central with me.

"I told her to keep an eye out for you," she adds, "but as you can imagine, there might be an intimidation factor with you being, well, who you are."

"And who is that?"

"You tell me."

"Touché. Are Charlie and I allowed to talk?"

"Of course, silly," Tracy says. "But I mean, obviously you can't, well—"

"I know!"

"I wanted to make sure you remember the rules." She gives me a look that suggests she has a long list at the ready of times when I didn't.

"How could I forget?"

"How's it going avoiding Audrey?" she inquires, changing the subject.

"It's okay, I guess."

"You guess?"

"I mean, I'm not dating her or anything, if that's what you're asking," I say defensively, like Audrey's not all I think about, and like we didn't recently share this incredibly complicated and challenging bonding experience together.

"If you can, keep things tickety-boo," Tracy says, patting me on the leg under the cover. "Let's get you through the year, and we're home free."

"This feels strange," I pop out. Because as annoying as she is, I miss the old Tracy. How we used to talk.

"What does?"

"This," I say. "You and me. It feels like we both have walls up or something."

"I think I see what you mean. I'm not sure what it is."

"Me neither."

"I don't think of you as a kid the way I did the past three years. You don't need me as much as you did before," she suggests.

"That's not true."

Tracy seems startled. "It isn't?" She smoothes the collar on her tunic. "You are growing up, Kyle. Changer or not, you're about to graduate and enter the real world."

"And you're about to start a family."

"Looks that way," she says, absently patting her stomach. "No putting the toothpaste back in the tube now."

"Are you talking about Mr. Crowell's sperm?" I joke.

Tracy squeals. "Kyle! Inappropriate!"

"You brought it up."

She grabs my toes through the blanket and wiggles. "You've always had that sense of humor. Since day one. Anyway, I've got to meet the realtor." She gets up to go.

"Good luck finding your dream home."

"You're doing well, Kyle," she offers, squinting. "Better than you realize."

"Thanks," I say. As she walks away, I yell after her, "Do the visions ever *not* happen at all?"

Tracy freezes. "It's impossible to know everything," she answers, unlike the last time I asked.

"You'd tell me if you knew, right?" I press.

But she's gone.

CHANGE 4-DAY 48

It was easy skipping Chronicling for a couple weeks after first ditching the Changers Mixer—with very little to no consequences, outside of a BS e-mail update I sent to Turner affirming how much I'm learning as Kyle, poster boy of traditional masculinity. Everybody—the Council, Tracy, even my dad—seems to be letting up the pressure on me during Y-4. Kyle, I guess, can do no wrong.

I don't really have an instinct to "process" anymore. My brain feels rejiggered. More set in the present. Introspection and regret largely a habit of the past. All is mad easy when you are Mr. Basic Wonderful, King of Bachelor Nation, making all-American dreams come true.

I keep reminding myself that I'm only hurting myself if I don't get my thoughts down in these Chronicles. So much is happening—so much has *happened* since I first changed into Drew—that I know I'll forget a lot when it comes time to make a decision about who I'm going to be for the rest of my life. I mean, that's like seven months away. I can't bear to think of it right now.

Well, well, what do we have here? Me reminding me to do the right thing, with nary a guilt trip from Tracy, or a stink eye from Dad. Who, by the way, was at long last inducted into the Council last week, and is spending more hours than ever at Changers HQ. Mom joking she's a Changers widow, but secretly she likes her alone time and has taken up doubles tennis with some friends she shares her therapy practice with.

To Dad, everything appears to be great on the outside with me—I'm the ideal son this year, winning football game after football game (yeah, I stayed on). I'm keeping the grades up, not getting distracted by dating anybody, much less Static-non-grata Audrey. No shaved head and black wardrobe, no running away from home to bunk with Radical Changers. No cloud of depression bumming everyone out. No Abider drama, or arrests, or out-and-proud marches.

Even Jason, my quarterback coach Abider-in-waiting, has become president and CEO of the Kyle Smith fan club. (What that says about Kyle I shudder to think.)

Anyway, the reason I came home and resumed Chronicling tonight is because of homecoming. Always drama at the homecoming.

First off, after my game (which we won, 35–10), I was so ragged all I wanted to do was stay home and finish season two of *The Fall*. But Andy begged me to hit the dance with him, because he'd never been to one and was still trying to mack on this sophomore girl he won't stop talking about, using me as his wingman. He said the girl reminds him of Destiny. (He's pathetic.)

That said, I sort of feel bad for Andy, seeing as his family members haven't called to check on him even once since we told them he was bunking with us, and all he ever does is go to school and then go to work on weekends, so he can "pay rent," even though my parents keep telling him that's crazy. Anyhow, the Andy guilt got me to go to a dance that triggered severe PTSD, but hey, what are friends for?

I barely dress up for it, throwing on a tie at the last minute when I realize a short-sleeve, button-down Hawaiian surf shirt probably isn't proper enough to get me in the door. Wish I could fit into that retro tuxedo I wore when I was Drew. I was so much cooler then. I actually cared about stuff. As Kyle, everything comes so easy, it's hard to care. But, whatever. (See what I mean?)

Andy is sporting an ill-fitting, boxy tuxedo that he rented for himself, and which Mom somehow made less tragic with a couple of hems and stitches. I add a fake flower to my shirt pocket, and some dorky blue suspenders with frogs on them, loud-ass socks, and shorts. The full Urkel. Technically I'm wearing a tie, so they can't keep me out.

Mom snaps a photo with her iPhone of Andy and me mugging in front of the fireplace, with Snoopy between us in sunglasses that keep falling off his thick head.

"Don't drink tonight," Dad says, handing me the keys to his car.

"Yep, got it," I say.

"I'll keep him out of the punch bowl," Andy promises, and it seems like it's the first time he's been mildly excited about anything for a long time.

Flash forward to the dance, where I instantly spot Audrey, mostly keeping to herself. Michelle Hu is there too, and I ask her to save me a slow jam, which makes her table full of fellow mathletes lose their collective brainiac minds. Michelle is chill though. She truly gives zero effs. (Every year I wonder why I don't spend more time with her. That girl's gonna be a senator or invent a new Internet someday, I'm sure of it.)

Chloe and her bees are predictably skulking around, making fun of other girls and saying "cute" like it's a curse word. And then there is Kris, being extra, even for him, costumed in a fabulous fitted leopard-print catsuit with a high-necked ruffled shirt underneath.

Stoner Jerry walks by. Stoned. "What's the haps?" he says to me, as Caden, my tight end, rolls up behind him.

"Dance, dance revolution," I joke with Jerry, who nods slowly.

"No doubt," he replies, carrying on his way.

"Why are you talking with that loser?" Caden says before Jerry is even out of earshot.

"Who says he's a loser?"

"Everyone who has ever looked at him for even two seconds," Caden spits. "You know, you don't *have* to talk with everybody, right? Wouldn't want people getting the wrong impression."

I want to ask him what impression that would be exactly, but Andy pops up, two Cokes in hand, bristling with anticipation about finding his latest infatuation. Caden saunters off, put off by yet another "loser" I don't know that I don't need to talk to.

"Okay, where is she?" I ask Andy, and he points across the room.

"Her?" I ask, spying a sweet, bespectacled white girl digging into a bag of popcorn. Not Andy's type, in my ample experience.

"No, the one in the blue skirt, by the cake. Isn't she gorgeous?"

I start laughing.

"What?" Andy asks, suddenly insecure. "You're being a dick."

"No, it's . . ." Of course he's crushing on Charlie, the only other Changer in school. We'd exchanged nods since Tracy filled me in about her, but both of us have tacitly kept our distance once we clocked one another.

I'm not sure what to do, like, can I tell him? I'm not supposed to be outing myself to Statics (Andy's not even supposed to be in on my identity), so outing another Changer is probably like fifty times worse of a cardinal offense than self-disclosure.

"She's really cute," I finally say, deciding to let it ride. "Let's go talk to her."

"Would you?" Andy asks, positively puppy-doggish. As we cross the room to chat up Charlie, I can't help but wonder what it is in Andy that keeps attracting him to Changers. He's got Changer radar. Chay-dar. (That's dumb.)

"This is my buddy Andy," I announce with faux formality when we arrive. "He's one awesome guy, and he's been crushing on you from afar, and so I was wondering if you'd do the honor of dancing with him, and at some point maybe even being seen in the daylight with him?"

Andy's face goes white, whispers, "Asshole," through his teeth.

"Radical honesty. It's what's for dinner," Charlie says, laughing, even seemingly somewhat charmed. So my job is clearly done here. Plus I have to take a leak.

On the way to the bathroom I grab a few mouthfuls of cookies, gulp them down with a swig of punch, which I can tell has miraculously NOT been spiked tonight—likely because Jason (the proverbial turd in every punch bowl ever) graduated from Central last year.

I'm at the urinal when Andy comes bursting in the bathroom door, hollering, "Kyle! Kyle!"

"What the hell, man?" I ask, the pee scared right back in me. "I thought I got you set up."

"You won! You won!" he shouts.

"Won what?"

"Homecoming king!"

"Stop messing with me, I wasn't even running," I say, zipping up.

"It's student vote, dumbass. I swear to whatever, they totally called your name. You need to get out there."

I'm sure you can guess who my homecoming queen is . . .

Chloe. Chlo-Jo. The Chlo Monster. Chlo-zilla. The girl who sets all other females back ten years every time she opens her mouth. When I come out of the john, she's already onstage, posing and arching her back like she's a movie star in front of a step-and-repeat at the Oscars. I walk up to join her, because that's what it seems like everybody is expecting me to do, and that's when I spot Audrey and Kris sarcastic-clapping from the side of stage as the tiara is placed on Chloe's head, then an even bigger, shinier crown on mine.

Everybody is hooting and whistling as we are forced to dance to "All My Life" by K-Ci & JoJo in the middle of the dance floor, and Chloe immediately adheres her body to mine like the aliens in, well, *Alien*. Attempting to suck the life out of me while we sway back and forth and everybody takes our photo and swoons and ostensibly wants to be us—although if they knew the real story of our lives, I think they might feel differently.

I catch a glimpse of Audrey making gagging faces to Kris. For his part, Kris goes full drag shade by flat-out ignoring Chloe and my existence entirely.

As the song switches to a Kesha number and people start filling in around us, Kris takes off for the bathroom, while Audrey plops down on the side of the stage, swinging her legs off the edge. She's so pretty tonight, and I would do almost anything to be dancing with her instead of the succubus who's still clinging to my torso and CURRENTLY TRYING TO SHOVE HER SLIPPERY SEA SLUG OF A TONGUE DOWN MY THROAT. She tastes like peach liqueur and breath mints, and seems oblivious to the fact that I might not want her saliva on my face. By the time I disentangle from my long Chlo-mare, I notice Audrey is gone.

"Are you a homo?" Chloe sneers at me, as I peel off to search for Audrey.

"What?" I say, frantically glancing around.

"There is no way you're into chicks if you aren't into me," she says, snickering to herself as she flicks the crown off my head. It tumbles down my body and onto the floor.

I kick it under a banquet table and hightail it out of there, rubbing Chloe's DNA off my lips as I go.

The halls are empty, some completely dark, everything eerily quiet. Rows and rows of lockers containing everybody's secrets. I peer down the freshman wing, and then the junior. Nada. Finally, in the pitch-black sophomore section, I think I can hear something. I head down, calling out: "Audrey?"

When I turn the corner past the chem lab, I spot two figures at the end of the hall—one big, with his back up against the lockers, and a smaller one kneeling in front. A part of me worries for a second that it might be Audrey, even though as I get closer it becomes unmistakable that it is a skinny dude kneeling in front of the other larger guy.

I start backing up to give them their privacy, but soon as I turn, the bigger guy hears my sneakers squeak and clocks me. I recognize immediately who it is: Buster, my offensive lineman, whose own parents would buy him a ticket to hell if they knew he digs guys.

"Faggot, get off me!" I hear Buster yell theatrically. He reaches down and grabs the skinny dude by the neck, hoists him up, and launches him into the lockers on the other side of the hallway. Poor guy slides like a rag doll to the floor. Buster quickly zips up his pants, marches over, and begins viciously kicking the guy curled on the ground.

Something in me snaps. I sprint over, tackling Buster. "What the hell are you doing?" I scream in his face, pinning him to the cold floor beneath me, my elbow across his neck.

"Get off!" he shouts, spittle flying onto my face.

I stay put, craning my neck to check on the second guy, and realize, *Oh god*, it's Kris, his lips split and bloody, a huge gash on the side of his skull. "Are you okay?" I ask him, as he struggles to stand, but can't seem to find his feet.

It's at this point that Buster frees an arm and sucker-

CHANGE 4-DAY 54

I don't think I've ever been knocked around so badly on a football field. This evening was by far the toughest team we played all season, and my body ached from the stripe on my helmet to the tips of my cleats by the time I hobbled off that field after those forty-eight minutes of play.

We managed to secure the victory in the last few seconds of the fourth quarter, when my third down, thirty-yard bullet into the end zone hit one of my receivers right in his outstretched hands—and you've never heard a high school stadium erupt like that. At least I never had.

I won't lie: this win felt good. I think because I had to work for every single yard we earned. And because it was the first playoff game of the postseason. Afterward, people were saying if we keep playing like this, we could maybe have a shot at winning the Tennessee State Championship.

Why do I care that people think we could win a state championship? No clue. But I do. Not even Jason did that during his four years as QB-1. A fact he keeps reminding me of at every opportunity. "With your arm and my mentorship, this could go all the way," he whispered to me as the last seconds of the game wound down and it was clear our opponents weren't going to be able to tie it back up with a touchdown. It's perpetually disorienting how much Jason needs me to need him.

After the referee's last whistle, my whole team rushed me, lifting me up and carrying me around the edge of the field like I was a conquering emperor returning from distant lands with the spoils of victory. Chloe and the other cheerleaders were handspringing maniacally across the field, maroon pom-poms flying everywhere and landing in little puffs on the grass. The color guard dudes sprinted around the track with their giant Central flags whipping in the wind behind them, and the marching band started blasting a kick-ass rendition of Daft Punk's "Get Lucky," which caused everybody in the stands to start rocking out in unison.

I could go on about the stats of the game, but in fifty years that's not what I'm going to remember. What I'm going to recall forever, no matter who I am in this world, is the feeling of being that guy atop the dog pile, the one everybody admires, is talking about, wants to be like—my teammates, grown-ass men, kids, women of all ages. It feels as if I could have anything I want right this minute. And that's a feeling that keeps feeding itself, like you're Ryan Gosling or Bruno Mars, and you can do no wrong (even though like every human you do a lot of wrong in your life), and everybody loves you everywhere you go, and you kind of can't help but let thoughts creep in: *Yeah, maybe I AM better than other people. I DO deserve everything I get!*

And from there it's not a far hop, skip, or jump over to: *And that person over there doesn't deserve it as much as I do.*

I could really get used to going through the world this way. Because I'm figuring out when you go through the world like Kyle, beloved and coddled, you only have to be one-tenth as good as a woman, or a person of color, or any person of difference, to be awarded ALL THE THINGS. I know this because, duh, I was a girl, and a person of color, and a kid who didn't fit any standard of "normal." Because I've read the experiments where they change names on identical resumes to sound "black" and those fake black people don't get interviews; where they slap a man's name on a woman's manuscript and it miraculously gets published; where they do blind tests on tech programmers and women come out ahead, but still can't get hired; where photos of plus-sized people are assigned all types of negative labels by kids, but the same exact people shrunken in the pictures are assigned nice qualities.

I know all of the above because, of course, I wasn't born this way. This white, straight, modern Greek god Adonis-being carried aloft and worshipped, his feet scarcely needing to touch the ground. And as I was up there watching the crowd blur by in the stands, shimmying and cheering, everybody giving me thumbs-up and patting my legs, basically pinning all of their hopes and dreams on my ability to lead a team to victory—all I could think of was that they would crap their pants if they knew.

Knew that merely fifty-five days ago, I had boobs. And a vagina. And wasn't white. Or "straight." Or skinny. Or blond. Nor really welcome to take part in any of these rituals. It dawned on me up there on everybody's shoulders that inhabiting Kyle feels like drag—drag that delivers every fantasy of masculinity these people ever had.

It's all too much to figure out, and anyway, who has the time, because after the local TV news sticks a camera in my face (the same reporter who covered the RaChas visibility march when I was Kim, in fact), the crowds on the sideline part, and a dude in all orange approaches me with a confident stride.

Turns out it's a college scout, and he barks, "Great game, great game, Kyle!" and extends his hand.

"Thank you, sir," I say, as more teammates, coaches, and fans tap me when they pass by, like they're touching the hem of Jesus' garment or something. This guy is acting as if he wants something from me, like I can really help him. And he can really help me. Like he holds all the answers to the universe beneath his bright-orange cap.

We shake hands. "I think there's quite a future waiting for you at Syracuse University," he asserts, leaning in, beads of sweat on his brow glimmering in the lights around the field. Behind him, there's another dude in a different shade of orange shirt and hat waiting to talk to me, and behind him, Audrey heading my way too. I haven't seen her since she stuck that letter in my locker, and all I want to do is ditch this circus, take her by the river, and tell her how brave that letter was, and how I want to be that brave too.

"You're busy," the Syracuse guy says, "but I'll be in touch. I will definitely be in touch."

And then the next recruiter sneaks in before Audrey can, grabs my hand, shakes vigorously. "Dave Daniels, Auburn, great to meet you."

"Kyle Smith," I say.

"Oh, we know who you are, son, we've had our eye on you all season. I'll let you go, but let's talk after the playoffs, okay?"

"Sure," I say, and smile at Audrey to alert her she's up next. (See? I'm already thinking like a celebrity, somebody even my friends need to line up to talk to.)

"Great job," Audrey says halfheartedly, once we're (semi) alone, albeit with a riot of celebration flowing around us.

"This is all really weird." I gesture toward the college scouts. "What'd they say?"

"They wanted directions to the nearest Chipotle."

"Don't joke. This is a really big deal," she says, punching my shoulder pad. "Trust me, I come from a football family."

As if on cue, one of my linemen jumps between Audrey and me, screams, "WOOOOOO!" at the top of his lungs, and then pours a cup of Gatorade over his head and crushes the empty cup against his forehead before running off.

"Wow," I say.

"Yeah, wow," Audrey echoes, while a few more people come up to congratulate me and I quickly thank them and try to communicate subtly through body language without seeming like a dick that I don't want to be interrupted. (*Don't look me in the eyes!*)

"I should let you go," she says. "But I wanted to congratulate you. That was a great pass."

"I got your letter," I blurt.

"Oh, okay. We're going *there*," she says, slowly bobbing her head.

"No, I m-mean," I stutter. Then regroup: "I didn't want you to think I was ignoring it."

"I didn't think you were ignoring it."

"Can I call you?"

"Sure."

"Okay, great," I say, relieved.

"Want my number?" she asks, her cheeks pinking up like they do when she's flustered.

I have to stop myself from saying, *I already have it on mental speed dial.* I just nod.

"Are you good at memorizing?" she asks, and I nod again, even though I'm not, and then she slowly speaks her phone number, three times in a row, to make sure I record it in my brain amidst the madness.

"I'll call you later!" I shout, as I'm dragged away again, this time by Coach Tyler, who is trying to gather the team around to take a knee so he can give us a quick postgame rundown, plus a stern warning that it's fine to celebrate the victory tonight, but we have five days of practice to prepare for the semifinals, and he wants our butts ready to go first thing Monday afternoon.

I might (presently) be a dumb jock, but I've learned one thing as Kyle: no post–football game house party is as fun as everybody thinks it's going to be. In fact, in my experience (and Drew's and Oryon's), they are the ultimate, terrifying proof of chaos theory in motion. Meaning, if one human brain has something like eighty billion neurons and a trillion synapses to misfire at any given time, multiply that by 150–200 brains at one party, raised by the factor of negative-zero parents chaperoning said party, and there is an ever-present, exponential possibility for outright tragedy to emerge from the air displaced by even a single beer burp (much less the flap of a butterfly's wing).

Translation: I headed straight home and went to bed after Coach Taylor released us.

I reread Audrey's letter five times before I fell asleep.

punches me right in the chin. The blow startles me, but it barely hurts, thanks to adrenaline and my essential Kyle alpha-maleness. I feel a very clear urge to beat Buster like a piñata, but I tamp it down, opting to body-check him back to the floor instead, hard enough that he loses his breath.

"Chill OUT!" I shout into his face. "Kris, are you okay?"

He still won't answer, but he's hoisted himself to a sitting position and is blotting his lip with a scarf from his pocket.

It's then that Audrey turns the corner and comes running down the hall, her fancy shoes clip-clop-echoing on the shiny linoleum. While I'm distracted at the sight of her, Buster somehow summons the strength to roll out from beneath me, scrambles to his feet, and bolts. Audrey hurries up, kneels next to Kris, gently touches his face.

"Oh my god, what happened?" she asks him, but he pushes her hand away.

"Nothing," Kris says, pulling himself upright and limping toward the bathroom.

"Let me help," Audrey coos, putting an arm around him as they walk.

"I just want to be alone!" Kris yells, shrugging off her arm and pushing into the first bathroom he comes to, the girls'.

Soon as the door closes behind Kris, Audrey asks me, "What. The. Hell. Happened?"

I don't answer either. Because how can I explain all of the psychological mechanics at play? Buster's self-loathing and fear of his desires. Kris's hunger to be wanted, even by someone who can't do it openly. How it doesn't matter how many kids identify as queer or nonbinary, there's still the so-called "normal" and the "not-normal," and the "normal" people get to decide how much "not-normal" they'll tolerate on any given day, in any given situation, and the effects of these two dynamics clashing are written all over Kris's battered face.

I know Audrey fancies herself a member of the club. But she's never fully come out, walked the walk, told her family and her friends and her church that she's bisexual, lesbian, pansexual, whatever. She's kept it close. And that's fine. But it is a far shout from someone like Kris who actually puts his life on the line every single day in order to roam the planet as himself. Or themself, which, if I had to guess, is where he's headed.

Kris lost his home, his family, because he wasn't willing to forfeit a single color from his crayon box. That takes guts. And heart. And fortitude. And grit. And this part I can tell Audrey.

"Kris will be fine," I say. "He's one of the strongest people I know."

CHANGE 4-DAY 52

Dear Kyle,

I hope you don't take this the wrong way, and that it's not too "Downton Abbey" that I'm writing you a letter, but I wanted to ask you something, and it seems like we never get more than a few passing seconds in homeroom or the hall to connect. I really find myself wanting to talk to you in more depth than those passing encounters can allow.

I know you're totally busy with (meathead) football and the playoffs, so I figured a note might be the easiest way to go, so you don't feel like you have to respond immediately, and can take your time to think about things before getting back to me. Or not getting back to me! Whatever you want.

Anyway, I don't really know how to say this, so I'm just going to say it, because I have a feeling from what I've seen in you that this wouldn't be taken as an insult. But I'm wondering: are you gay? I'm not sure if you know this, but rumors are being spread by Buster and Chloe that you are. I don't trust rumors. And by the way, it's TOTALLY cool if you are gay, I am 100% down with that. In fact, if I'm being honest, I'm pretty much bisexual, since my last relationship was with a girl. And before that a guy, and before that another girl ... which I can't

believe I'm telling you since I've never told anyone before. But this note is about taking that leap of trust. I
want you to feel like you can be honest with me if you feel
comfortable. And there will be no judgment.

Because here's why I'm asking: I like you. Like, really, really like you.

You're a good guy, Kyle. I can tell about these things.

For some reason—don't freak out—I feel very connected to you. And I can't help but feel that you feel some
connection to me too. Please tell me if I'm wrong. (I can
take it, I'm a big girl! I've lived through some shit, trust
and believe.) But I don't want to keep pretending I don't
feel something I do.

A dear friend showed me once that keeping secrets
makes you sick. And that life is shorter than we think.
I know I would always wonder, if I didn't at least try
with you. So this is me, trying.

xo,
Audrey

p.s. You did a really good thing for Kris the other night.
There's something about you that makes me feel safe.

CHANGE 4-DAY 54

I don't think I've ever been knocked around so badly on a football field. This evening was by far the toughest team we played all season, and my body ached from the stripe on my helmet to the tips of my cleats by the time I hobbled off that field after those forty-eight minutes of play.

We managed to secure the victory in the last few seconds of the fourth quarter, when my third down, thirty-yard bullet into the end zone hit one of my receivers right in his outstretched hands—and you've never heard a high school stadium erupt like that. At least I never had.

I won't lie: this win felt good. I think because I had to work for every single yard we earned. And because it was the first playoff game of the postseason. Afterward, people were saying if we keep playing like this, we could maybe have a shot at winning the Tennessee State Championship.

Why do I care that people think we could win a state championship? No clue. But I do. Not even Jason did that during his four years as QB-1. A fact he keeps reminding me of at every opportunity. "With your arm and my mentorship, this could go all the way," he whispered to me as the last seconds of the game wound down and it was clear our opponents weren't going to be able to tie it back up with a touchdown. It's perpetually disorienting how much Jason needs me to need him.

After the referee's last whistle, my whole team rushed me, lifting me up and carrying me around the edge of the field like I was a conquering emperor returning from distant lands with the spoils of victory. Chloe and the other cheerleaders were handspringing maniacally across the field, maroon pom-poms flying everywhere and landing in little puffs on the grass. The color guard dudes sprinted around the track with their giant Central flags whipping in the wind behind them, and the marching band started blasting a kick-ass rendition of Daft Punk's "Get Lucky," which caused everybody in the stands to start rocking out in unison.

I could go on about the stats of the game, but in fifty years that's not what I'm going to remember. What I'm going to recall forever, no matter who I am in this world, is the feeling of being that guy atop the dog pile, the one everybody admires, is talking about, wants to be like—my teammates, grown-ass men, kids, women of all ages. It feels as if I could have anything I want right this minute. And that's a feeling that keeps feeding itself, like you're Ryan Gosling or Bruno Mars, and you can do no wrong (even though like every human you do a lot of wrong in your life), and everybody loves you everywhere you go, and you kind of can't help but let thoughts creep in: *Yeah, maybe I AM better than other people. I DO deserve everything I get!*

And from there it's not a far hop, skip, or jump over to: *And that person over there doesn't deserve it as much as I do.*

I could really get used to going through the world this way. Because I'm figuring out when you go through the world like Kyle, beloved and coddled, you only have to be one-tenth as good as a woman, or a person of color, or any person of difference, to be awarded ALL THE THINGS. I know this because, duh, I was a girl, and a person of color, and a kid who didn't fit any standard of "normal." Because I've read the experiments where they change names on identical resumes to sound "black" and those fake black people don't get interviews; where they slap a man's name on a woman's manuscript and it miraculously gets published; where they do blind tests on tech programmers and women come out ahead, but still can't get hired; where photos of plus-sized people are assigned all types of negative labels by kids, but the same exact people shrunken in the pictures are assigned nice qualities.

I know all of the above because, of course, I wasn't born this way. This white, straight, modern Greek god Adonis-being carried aloft and worshipped, his feet scarcely needing to touch the ground. And as I was up there watching the crowd blur by in the stands, shimmying and cheering, everybody giving me thumbs-up and patting my legs, basically pinning all of their hopes and dreams on my ability to lead a team to victory—all I could think of was that they would crap their pants if they knew.

Knew that merely fifty-five days ago, I had boobs. And a vagina. And wasn't white. Or "straight." Or skinny. Or blond. Nor really welcome to take part in any of these rituals. It dawned on me up there on everybody's shoulders that inhabiting Kyle feels like drag—drag that delivers every fantasy of masculinity these people ever had.

It's all too much to figure out, and anyway, who has the time, because after the local TV news sticks a camera in my face (the same reporter who covered the RaChas visibility march when I was Kim, in fact), the crowds on the sideline part, and a dude in all orange approaches me with a confident stride.

Turns out it's a college scout, and he barks, "Great game, great game, Kyle!" and extends his hand.

"Thank you, sir," I say, as more teammates, coaches, and fans tap me when they pass by, like they're touching the hem of Jesus' garment or something. This guy is acting as if he wants something from me, like I can really help him. And he can really help me. Like he holds all the answers to the universe beneath his bright-orange cap.

We shake hands. "I think there's quite a future waiting for you at Syracuse University," he asserts, leaning in, beads of sweat on his brow glimmering in the lights around the field. Behind him, there's another dude in a different shade of orange shirt and hat waiting to talk to me, and behind him, Audrey heading my way too. I haven't seen her since she stuck that letter in my locker, and all I want to do is ditch this circus, take her by the river, and tell her how brave that letter was, and how I want to be that brave too.

"You're busy," the Syracuse guy says, "but I'll be in touch. I will definitely be in touch."

And then the next recruiter sneaks in before Audrey can, grabs my hand, shakes vigorously. "Dave Daniels, Auburn, great to meet you."

"Kyle Smith," I say.

"Oh, we know who you are, son, we've had our eye on you all season. I'll let you go, but let's talk after the playoffs, okay?"

"Sure," I say, and smile at Audrey to alert her she's up next. (See? I'm already thinking like a celebrity, somebody even my friends need to line up to talk to.)

CHANGE 4-DAY 55

I waited till eleven, then picked my way across the messy floor on heavy, sore legs, locked myself in the bathroom, and dialed Audrey. She picked up her phone after one ring, whispered, "Hold on," and presumably headed somewhere for some privacy from her family too, the forbidden young lovers of the Montague and Capulet households back in action!

"How are you feeling?" I ask after she returns to the line.

"I should be asking *you* that," she says. "My brother hasn't stopped peacocking around the house in nothing but his ripped old Central jersey and tight-ass performance briefs. Like he was the one who threw that last touchdown."

"I think he believes he did."

"I can't wait for his knee rehab to be over so he can go the hell off to college and be somebody else's problem." I can tell she's outside, because it sounds like a big truck roars by. "Blergh, I don't want to talk about him now. Sooooo . . ."

"So," I say.

"So."

Our familiar pattern. She doesn't know how familiar it is.

"I wanted to talk to you about the letter," I say then.

"Too much?"

"No!"

"Oh, phew. I considered throwing it away without giving it to you."

"That would've been a national disaster."

"Remains to be seen."

"Okay, so I . . ." I begin to say, before stalling out.

This is it. Here's the line. I see it right in front of me. And now I have to decide whether to cross that line. Right here, right now.

Audrey is quiet. I think I hear her soft breathing on the other end of the line. I can feel a rush of sweat in my pits, on the palms of my hands.

"Uh. Well, I guess I wanted to say that you're right. I *am* afraid of something."

"Oh?"

"And there is something holding me back," I continue. "But that's not your problem. It's my problem. And I'll figure it out."

"Okay, wow," she says. It seems like that wasn't what she was prepared to hear from me.

"Anyway . . ." I can feel my heart pounding through my rib cage. You know what? *Fuck it.*

FUCK.

IT.

I can be with Audrey and not reveal who I am.

We're connected in some strange, inevitable way anyhow. What's the difference whether she knows who I am or not? She's drawn to me, so why does it matter *why* she's drawn to me? I've been Kyle long enough that I know how to stay in check. If I can lead a team to a football championship, I can avert some stupid kiss vision. Besides, Tracy said it may not even be what it seems to be. Maybe the crash is a metaphor. Or a red herring. It must be, because come hell or high water, I could never act in a way that would enrage Audrey to that point.

Fate can't play out if you already know what's supposedly going to happen. Like, if I know a deer is supposed to jump out from this tree at this exact time, on this exact road, I won't go down that road. Problem solved.

And let's say, for the sake of argument, I find myself on the road regardless, and I'm about to come upon that time and place in the road where I know the deer is supposed to jump out: I can always slam on the brakes.

I am in control of my life. My lives are not in control of me.

And when it comes time to pick my Mono, maybe Kyle will need to be sacrificed (regardless of how good it feels living a life like his). Or maybe he won't. I don't have to decide that this instant. All I know is what I know. That I love this girl, and she loves me, and she knew about the whole Changer thing and was mostly unfazed by it, and so nothing will tear us asunder. Not even so-called prophesy or kismet or whatever you want to call it.

So I clear my throat, speak right into the phone so there can be no confusion in the matter whatsoever, and say: "Audrey, will you go out with me?"

WINTER

SPRING

CHANGE 4-DAY 240

I thought I could stay a step ahead of the future.
I thought I could beat back fate.
  I was wrong.

CHANGE 4-DAY 241

At least she's alive.

One tiny gift that the universe has seen fit to bestow.

She's alive. On life support, but alive.

Audrey's in a coma.

There's swelling in her brain, and it's threatening to cause permanent damage. There's nowhere for a swollen brain to go. The skull is a finite place, even if the mind is not.

I'm staring at her from the left side of her hospital bed. It's three a.m. and the nurse has let me sneak in to visit again tonight, thanks to Elyse who has a friend at Vanderbilt who knew somebody who works nights in the ER. (Nobody but immediate family members are allowed in ICU.) The drone of the ventilator is eerie; it whistles and sounds wholly antithetical to what life really sounds like, and I hate it. But it is one of the only things keeping Audrey with us.

She just lies there. Doesn't feel anything, not when they periodically scrape the bottom of her feet or rub their knuckles across her breast bone. A part of her head is shaved, and there is a pressure monitor sticking through a hole in her skull into her brain. She has five other tubes coming in and out of her. Maybe it's four. Or six. A feeding tube, catheter, IV, some other things I can't even identify. Tight stockings to prevent blood clots. Her legs so thin and wiry under the institutional white sheet.

It seems dire, like she could slip away at any time, but Eylse's nurse friend assures me it's better for her to be in this coma for the time being, and everything's completely normal in light of what Audrey's brain went through in the car wreck. *After what I put her brain through*, I'm thinking as the nurse talks in a hushed tone, in case Audrey can hear. Which it's hard to believe she can, but they keep telling me to talk to her as much as possible, even though it seems like she can't hear anything. So I do.

I read articles from her favorite magazines to her. I narrate the plots of her favorite John Hughes movies: *The Breakfast Club. Pretty in Pink. Some Kind of Wonderful.* I bring in books of poetry and try to get through each one without crying at the beauty some writers are able to capture in a single line.

I tell her about all the things we've done together over the years. Cheerleading, bowling, karaoke, acting out the scene from *Romeo and Juliet*, working on the project about love for the *Peregrine Review* lit mag. Our first kiss.

The nurse tells me Audrey's ICP (intracranial pressure) is dropping ever so slightly. Another small gift. So I just keep reading her stories.

How has she ended up lying here in this bed like this? How could I have allowed it to happen? I was so selfish, full of hubris. I chose to risk her life rather than be apart from her for a year—one measly year in the grand scheme of things. I was too arrogant to think I would fail. I couldn't let her life play out without me. And now we're here.

I might as well confess it all, with this Chronicling

chip turned back on. If I don't get some of this stuff out somewhere, I might explode. Or head back to the bridge I thought about hurling myself off on C4–D1. I feel so helpless sitting aside while Audrey's lungs mechanically rise and fall in syncopation with the beeps from a monitor. Might as well Chronicle. It's my only therapy. And I should always have this record and thus never be allowed to forget what my ego allowed to happen to the person I love most.

I thought it would work, but obviously it didn't, and it sounds even stupider thinking about it now. But I guess I thought that dropping out of Changers life would somehow help me stay under the radar moving forward. Would muddle up what was "supposed" to happen. Would make me less a Changer, somehow. As Kyle, it was already so easy. My other V's had been such struggles. But as Kyle, I never had to do anything I didn't want to. (Except avoid Audrey.)

So, right after Audrey and my first official date—my first official date with Audrey when I was Kyle—Mom, Dad, and I were invited over to see Tracy and Mr. Crowell's new house, and to celebrate the impending birth with an intimate baby shower. Gifts, snacks, nonalcoholic champagne, and what seemed like a thousand helium balloons that Tracy explicitly forbade us from inhaling. Because "this isn't that kind of party."

While there, all I could think about was Audrey and when I could see her next, now that we were back on like Donkey Kong. I tried to join in the baby shower activities; listened to the teary toasts from Mr. Crowell's parents, even gave a lame one myself; ate some shrimp cocktail, drank a pink lemonade spritzer. There were even baby-inspired creative activities, where I found myself being art-directed by Tracy, who was trying to control what all of us were putting on the white cotton onesies that were laid out on the dining room table for guests to draw designs on with permanent markers. I drew a 'roided-out body on mine, in skimpy red bikini underwear, like a bodybuilding muscle-head, which Mr. Crowell chuckled at, but of course it positively horrified Tracy as being "vulgar."

While everybody finished their onesies, I subtly peeled off to take a tour around the new digs. I couldn't help my mind wandering to whether there was ever going to be a time when Audrey and I were moving in together, Static and Changer, with a baby on the way. Maybe that was premature—I mean, duh, of course it was, but I couldn't imagine ever being with anybody else . . .

The nurse just tottered in and hung a fresh IV bag.

CHANGE 4-DAY 241, PART TWO

So, except for the kitchen and living room, which were set up impeccably for the party, Mr. Crowell and Tracy were still only half moved in to the rest of the house, boxes and suitcases everywhere, piles of clothes on hangers slung over chairs, newspaper and bubble wrap strewn about. (Mr. Crowell's stuff, I'm certain. Tracy does not abide disorder.) In the bedroom, I spotted a flicker of light off a mirrored jewel box on the dresser, and upon closer examination, I saw that it had the Changers emblem etched into the glass on top. For some reason, I felt drawn to peek inside. I know, not cool, and Tracy would freak the eff out if she knew I was messing with her private things, but that's what I did. (She might want to get used to no privacy if she's about to have a child, but whatever.)

I flipped open the top of the box and looked inside. At first it seemed to be filled with a bunch of pins that the Council had given Tracy for various levels of service to the Changers cause, almost like Girl Scout badges or something, but then I saw it: that Barbie-sized little flashlight-y doodad. The fob that Tracy used each year to reboot and initialize my Chronicling chip on the morning of each new V—which triggers the Chronicling for the new year.

I picked up the thingamabob, and it beeped twice, then flashed blue. I glanced around to make sure nobody heard the beeping. And that's when the idea popped into my head. Maybe from watching too many intricately orchestrated heist movies, where some nerd with a personality disorder always had to devise a way to jam a signal temporarily so that the vaguely psychopathic but good-at-their-job crooks can breach some sort of security laser beam between them and their intended target.

Why not try that on myself? Redirect the future. Turn it off while I'm Kyle, get it back up and running soon as the danger's past.

So I stuck my thumb over the tip of the fob like I'd seen Tracy do four times before; it beeped again, flashed red a few times, and then I held it over the skin on the back of my neck where my Chronicling chip is implanted.

Exactly like those mornings of C1–D1, C2–D1, C3–D1, and C4–D1, it beeped once more, and then I felt a slight click and a whirr at the base of my skull, and then *whoosh*. Something was immediately different. Maybe not different, more like back to normal again, as in back when I was Ethan (and didn't have a rice-sized electronic chip implanted in the flesh at base of my neck!). So I tried thinking something to Chronicle, but after waving that fob over the chip, it didn't happen. Like that muscle stopped working or something.

I was offline. It felt free.

Thinking back, I vaguely remember Benedict talking about something like this, a hack on our Chronicling chips that some of the RaChas who went AWOL from their families would do, hoping to avoid Chronicling, but also to gum up the processes going on inside our bodies when gearing up for the next change, to try to stave it off. I never heard of it working, but Benedict did say that he knew one Changer a few years ago who managed to remove his chip himself. Sounds gruesome, sure, but at that point I understood the impulse. I would try anything to be able to unplug and live under the radar and basically not be a Changer who's beholden to Changers rules and life processes for the rest of Y-4, so I could be with Audrey and not have to worry about a vision that was part of Changers world, and not the real one.

Then I heard what I thought was somebody coming down the hall into the bedroom, so I quickly tucked the fob back into the little box, closed the lid, and shoved my hands in my pockets like I was admiring the new master bedroom with en suite bath—right in time for Mr. Crowell to pop his head in and say, "Hey, buddy, we're doing the cake," a little confused as to why I might be creeping around his bedroom solo.

"This is a dope house," I chirped, "love that vintage tile in the shower."

"Cool, thanks," he replied, jovial and floppy-haired as ever, as we went back down the hall and cut the *Congratulations* cake with the rest of the party.

And then I went home. Things felt a shade different. I can't describe how. But I wanted to test myself, beyond the not-Chronicling thing. I know it sounds crazy, and rather drastic, and anybody monitoring this might call the mental health authorities, but this was how desperately I wanted to escape the reality of who I was in that moment. I took my Swiss Army Knife, rubbed some alcohol on the blade, and cut into the skin on my thigh—to see how long the incision would take to heal: the usual one to two weeks it takes for Statics to heal from a cut like this, or the two to three days it takes a Changer. I figured once my Changer-ness was sort of jammed by my chip being turned off, then maybe my other Changer properties—like healing from injuries and illness quicker than Statics—would also get deactivated.

It was surprisingly easy to do, dragging that blade across the top of my thigh (I did it so my boxer briefs would cover the wound, so that my mom or Andy or anyone else wouldn't ask about it). Watching the first line of blood emerge, my whole body involuntarily shivered, so I ended up cutting a slightly longer line than I'd planned, maybe it was two inches total. Not that deep. Nothing horror film worthy.

I went into the bathroom and pressed some gauze onto the cut, and when it stopped bleeding, I smushed a little antibiotic ointment inside and covered the wound with a couple Band-Aids.

Satisfied that my secret science experiment was underway, I called Audrey and made another date with her. And another and another and another.

From then on, the months were perfect and blissful and radiant, like we were falling in love all over again, only this time in the pages of a J.Crew catalog. We spent every free second with each other, went to hole-in-the-wall restaurants in Nashville, walked by the river where, unbeknownst to Audrey, we'd already had sex (Kim), and even started hanging out a little with Michelle and Kris. Building a "normal" high school life together as a couple.

One weekend Aud, Kris, and I all went to Dolly Parton Drag night at the Carousel (this being Tennessee, one might argue that every night is Dolly Parton Drag night at the Carousel). We danced naughtily with drag queens, drag kings, boys, girls, and every amazing place in between.

I kept all this from Tracy and my folks, of course. Tracy was in pregnancy zone, which for her meant enrolling in every prenatal class ever invented, keeping her preoccupied and out of my hair. My mom and dad (Dad mostly) seemed so fracking over the moon about big-man-on-campus Kyle that they gave me more rope than ever.

As Kyle I projected authority, or rather it was projected on me. People expected I was handling my business, because that's what good-looking white guys do, right? It was peculiar, all this unwarranted benefit of the doubt, but I wasn't about to turn it away. I soaked in that privilege like a sponge. What was the alternative? Lock myself in a box and seal the lid shut?

It wasn't like I was becoming Jason, (the soggy piece of toast you can't wash down the drain). Yes, I had power now. I was the top of the social food chain. But I knew power came with responsibilities. I've seen *Spider-Man*. I wasn't throwing my dick around. Not even literally. Like, I wasn't pushing Audrey to have sex with me. After the whole roofie incident with April and Jenny, and Audrey getting dragged into cleaning up Jason's mess with me, sex was pretty much the last thing I wanted to bring into the mix. Plus, I'd had sex with her before, so that constant urge toward discovering somebody in that way had been satisfied (at least on my side). There *were* major make-out sessions. (I'm not a monk. Nor is Audrey.)

It turned out my cut took a good week to heal (kind of in between the Static and Changer healing rates, in my scientific conclusion about the experiment), so I posited that jamming my chip did in fact succeed in causing something to be "off" with my overall Changer-ness, and everything was so good between me and Audrey and life as Kyle in general that I used that one-week healing time to convince myself that I was practically a Static, inoculated against anything that could ever happen in Changerworld.

As if I needed more convincing, I took a hit in the second quarter of the championship football game a few weeks after Audrey and I started seeing one another. It wasn't too monster of a hit, but when my helmet slammed onto the grass beneath two heavy defensive linemen, I immediately heard a *pop*, then ringing in my ears, and then the coaches reluctantly (honestly, their faces looked like they were at their grandpappy's funeral or something) made me sit out the rest of the game because they thought I had a concussion.

I was so high on Audrey, and she was so high on me, that I didn't even really care that we lost the championship game after I got benched, because my backup QB Darryl couldn't pull off the win. There were some crushed faces in the stadium that night; Jason's was probably the most devastated of all of them, like his dreams had been dashed anew, but through me. Sorry. Not sorry. Yeah, it sucked to lose after working all season long toward this one massive collective dream that didn't get fulfilled. But it was not going to be the highlight of my life, and I knew it. I had bigger fish to fry.

On the way back to Genesis from the stadium in Knoxville where the championship game was played, Audrey and

I held hands in the rear of Kris's car. I rested my concussed head on Audrey's shoulder as the lights flashed by on the highway. My head throbbed, in addition to the ringing. The on-site doctor said I needed to go see my regular doctor on Monday, because some signs of concussion don't appear for up to a couple of days after an injury, though I'd decided I wasn't going to tell my parents what happened unless it got worse. And every sign that I was hurting like a Static proved my stupid hypothesis that pulling out of Changer-world would prevent the inevitable from actually happening.

I could see a rectangle of light on Kris's eyes in the rear-view mirror as he drove. He kept switching back and forth between us and the road ahead. Then he turned down the eighties new wave mix he was playing on the stereo.

"Calling all you basic bitches, I have an announcement," he said out of nowhere.

"You have a new boyfriend?" Audrey shot back.

"Girl, no. Bigger."

"Bigger than booing up?" she said.

"I'm transitioning."

"Oh my god!" Audrey screamed, bolting up beside me. "Yaaaaaasss!"

"Soon as I graduate and turn eighteen, I can get an appointment to see about hormones," Kris explained.

"This is amazing, I'm so happy for you," Audrey squealed, launching between the front seats and hugging Kris, making us swerve onto the shoulder of the road.

"That's so cool," I added, trying to tamp down the rush of feeling that raced through my heart for Kris. I was, of course, filled with pride because I knew he'd been struggling with this particular question and battling with his parents over it for a long time. But I was trying not let it show too blatantly. Because, of course, Kyle didn't know any of this.

"Should we start using *she* now?" I asked.

"I don't know," Kris said, sort of thrown by the question. Or maybe not by the question, but by the questioner.

"Well, we've got your back—in the bathroom, on the streets, whatever you want. Say the word," I offered, as Audrey settled back into me and I put my arm around her.

After another mile or so of driving in the dark, Kris said, "Okay, we figured me out. Let's figure *you* out."

"Who, me?" I asked.

"Yeah, you."

"What's to figure out?" Audrey said, pecking my sweaty cheek. "Mmm, salty."

"Why are you, cis poster child Aryan dream, driving back from the pinnacle of your high school career with a lifelong homo-soon-to-be-transgirl, and going out with a rumored lesbo?" he asked, smiling.

"Yeah, he really turned me into a *hasbian*, didn't he?" Audrey joked.

"I'm serious," Kris said. "Doesn't this wig you out at all?"

"What?" I said.

"This. Me, the drag bar, all the queeny stuff."

"Why would it wig me out?" I asked, knowing exactly why, if I'd been Kyle forever.

"Do you *know* any trans people?" Kris asked.

"He's from Seattle," Audrey interjected.

I understood Kris's doubts and suspicions, his apprehension about me. I mean, guys who look like Kyle have essentially made his life hell since the minute he was a conscious person in the world.

"So none of this makes you *uncomfortable*?" Kris continued. "Just asking."

"Well, you don't have to be such a bitch while doing it," Audrey said.

I liked her getting a little protective of me.

"Why would somebody being who they are make me uncomfortable?" I asked. "Cis white silence equals violence, right?"

Audrey beamed like a spotlight. At that, Kris shut up. I caught a glimpse of the corner of his mouth curling up in the rearview mirror, and then Audrey leaned close to my ear and whispered so only I could hear, "I love you."

An orderly just stopped by to restock a drawer of electrode pads for the EKG machine. He smiled feebly the way you do at friends and family of a coma patient, and then ducked back out of the room pushing his little cart with the wobbly left-rear wheel.

CHANGE 4-DAY 241, PART THREE

Flash forward a few months, and my mom and dad inform me that Andy and I were going to be on our own the following weekend. Dad's headed to a Changers Council retreat, where he will no doubt be regaling them with tales of Kyle's glory and how we can all anticipate me picking Kyle as my Mono so I can #saveusall if and when the Abider Armageddon comes. Mom's attending an Evolution of Psychotherapy conference in Atlanta.

All of which added up to me telling Andy he needed to take Snoopy and find a place for them to crash so Audrey and I could have the place to ourselves on Saturday night. I didn't care if it was a Motel 6, I told him. I'd pay.

So Audrey and I are hanging out at the coffee shop after school on the Wednesday before the weekend when I say, "So, uh, I was wondering whether you had any plans on Saturday night."

"Only to be with you," she says.

"I mean like *all* of Saturday night. My folks are going to be out of town . . ." I trail off in a way that I hope doesn't sound like I'm assuming anything.

"And . . ."

"And . . . I guess I was wondering whether you might like to stay over at my place that evening. With me."

"Bold. I like it." She cocks her head, as though considering me anew. Is she remembering when I asked her to sleep over at my place when my parents were out of town before? When it was at the old apartment, and I was of course Oryon, and instead of doing it in person, I wrote her a note, promising I would even sleep on the couch so as to seem nonthreatening, and that I only wanted to watch old movies and eat buttery popcorn on the couch with her all night long? We know where that led . . .

As if on cue, she abruptly asks, "Have you heard about this, like, new type of people called Changers?"

At this I spew coffee all across my lap.

Audrey jumps up to help me with a wad of napkins. She blots at my stomach, my pants, dangerously close to my crotch.

"It's okay, I'm good, I'm good, it was just too hot," I say, freaking the hell out inside but trying not to show it. Why is she bringing this up now? She must've been flashing back to the night with Oryon too.

"Yeah, so anyway, I was reading this, uh, guy's blog online, and there was a story about this community of people who are starting to live more openly. It's really actually incredible. They live as different people during each year of high school."

"Nope, never heard of them," I say. "Like, they wear costumes?"

"No. They *become* other people. It's a genetic mutation or something. I get it sounds crazy."

"Not as crazy as you think. I watch *Orphan Black*," I say.

"There aren't a lot of them," she continues, "but they had a march last spring in downtown Nashville."

"Cool." *Was this a test? Was I passing?*

"And yes, by the way," she then adds.

"Yes what?"

"Yes, I'll sleep over with you on Saturday night."

And that is another line I saw before me, toed, considered crossing—but this time decided NOT to. Which was another fateful decision. The decision that ended us up here in this ICU suite at Vanderbilt Medical Center. Because of course she was picking up on something, and that prompted me to think once more about coming clean and spilling all, telling Audrey I was Kim (Oryon, Drew), and the reason I never told you was because I had a vision from your future where Kyle makes you so angry that you get into a seemingly fatal car accident.

I should've dumped the information on her right then and there. Given her the power to decide whether or not to keep seeing me, whether she wanted to take the risk of the vision coming true. And then the two of us could have been on the lookout for circumstances that would bring about a fight like that. Two of us could've been ready to slam on the brakes and avoid the deer.

But no. I wanted to have this weekend with her. I knew that telling her would mess it up, so I put it off. Told myself I'd do it another time. Not realizing that there might not be another time.

Of course the night was perfect. (I'm not going to record details here, because it feels further messed up to do so while Audrey lies unconscious in the hospital bed next to me.) Before we drifted off to sleep sometime in the wee hours of the morning, Audrey gazed at me with such trust and complete recognition, even if all the pieces weren't visibly there before her. It was that Aristotle quote come to life: *Love is composed of a single soul inhabiting two bodies.* Or, ah, five.

In the morning, I rolled out of bed to go to pee while I thought Audrey was still asleep, so I didn't bother covering up my Changer brand like I did when I was Oryon two years ago, hurriedly pulling on my boxers when I went to get us drinks (before she found the charm bracelet that tipped her off and blew up the rest of our year together). I guess I was lulled into a comfort zone, because this time around, Audrey's charm bracelet was piled safely and in the open on my bedside table, next to her watch and other jewelry. There was nothing to discover.

When I come back to the room, though, she's sitting up against the wall. "What's that mark on your butt?" she asks casually, as I slip back into bed under the blanket with her.

"What?" I dodge.

"That scar on your left butt cheek."

"Which?" I stall. "Oh yeah, that's from when I used to play baseball and I slid into home one time and my pants ripped on some rocks. Skinned off half my cheek!" *This can't be happening. This is not happening. I am in control here.*

"You used to play baseball?"

"Yep, but then I decided to focus on football. For the chicks. Ha ha."

She pulls a peculiar expression.

Quick, distract: "Let's go to Waffle House for breakfast and then come back and get into bed."

She is thinking about it.

"What do you say?" I prompt.

After a little longer: "All righty."

She seems satisfied . . . enough.

We get dressed. I grab my wallet, keys to the house. "Meet you at the car," I say, hitting the bathroom to quickly brush my teeth. I assume she knows I mean her parents' car, which she'd driven over the night before and parked on the street. Not my parents' car, which she probably thought was in the garage. Which it wasn't. It was with my dad, who drove it to the Changers compound after dropping Mom at the airport.

But Audrey went to the garage anyway.

When I come out of the bathroom, I expect to feel stillness in the house, but there is a presence, and I sense it. Audrey is not waiting for me in her car. She is still inside. Her face white.

"Whose old scooter is that?" she asks when I turn the hallway corner.

"Mine," I say.

"Where'd you get it?"

"Uh, what do you mean?"

"Where did you get that scooter?" she asks again, her voice trembling.

"I—"

"Where?"

"I bought it off this girl on Craigslist last year," is the first thing I can think of.

"What girl?"

"I don't know, this nice Asian girl, I don't remember her name," I stammer.

"I knew it, I knew it. I knew, I knew, I knew." She pounds a closed fist against the wall in time with her words.

"Aud, let me—"

"I knew that was the same scar he had, but I thought it was from a skateboarding accident. And yours isn't from baseball. I KNEW it. Why are you lying to me? WHY?"

"Audrey, please, let me ex—"

"You promised you wouldn't lie to me. You, Kim, you promised me. You said you'd tell me on the first day of school, and you didn't. You LIED to me over and over and over again!" She is pretty much screaming, heading back toward my bedroom. "And why is there a dog bowl in the kitchen if there's no goddamn dog living here?"

The door to my bedroom slams.

There I am, watching everything unravel, but I refuse to believe this is actually happening again. My personal Groundhog Day from hell. I take a deep breath, remind myself I am in control of what happens and, more importantly, what doesn't happen. Put on the brakes, Kyle.

I creep, listen at my door. I can hear rustling, jingling, a few footsteps on the rug. I realize she's packing up her stuff. So I take three more deep breaths, in and out, steady, long, centering. *This will not turn into a fight. Keep her in the house.*

I knock gently.

"No!"

"Audrey, please."

"Go away!"

"Please, please let me say a few things," I say calmly, "and then you can go."

The door opens. "What could you possibly have to say

that I would ever believe again? You're a liar, Kyle. Kim, Oryon, Drew—whoever the hell you are. You are ALL liars."

She tries to slam the door again, but I block it with my hand. "Just hear me out, let me explain why I didn't tell you everything."

"You mean why you LIED?" Audrey says, gripping her keys between her fingers like a weapon.

"Five minutes."

"Fine."

"Do you want to sit down?"

"You have four minutes and fifty-five seconds left," she says, still standing.

"Okay." I take a seat on the messed-up bed. "Okay."

"Four minutes and fifty seconds."

"Yes. I am Drew, Oryon, and Kim, that's 100 percent true," I start. "But when I woke up as Kyle that first morning of school, I realized you were in danger, and I couldn't tell you I was Kyle, because I had to protect you from that danger."

"You mean you saw who you were, and what you looked like, and didn't want to be stuck from the jump with a girlfriend?" she seethes. "I can't believe I fell for this. I can't believe I fell for YOU."

"Come on, Audrey. It's always been you. It'll always be you."

"I don't believe you. Why would I believe you?"

"I'm telling you, it was too dangerous to reveal myself," I say, my voice rising.

"Dangerous how?"

I'm not sure how to answer. I need to keep her from freaking out completely.

"So this supposed *danger* suddenly went away when you took me out on that first date?" she presses.

"No, it's still there." I realize how flaky this all sounds. "I was trying to stay away from you so this thing wouldn't happen, but I couldn't. I couldn't handle not being with you."

"You sound like you're auditioning for a telenovela."

"Hear me out. Changers, like I told you before, aren't supposed to be with other Changers. We are supposed to be with sympathetic Statics, non-Changers like you. It's the whole mission."

"Mission?"

"Honestly? Yes. And then when a Changer-Static couple has a kid, that kid will most likely be a Changer. The idea being, eventually, centuries into the future, there will enough people on this planet who have lived multiple lives, who will have empathy and wisdom, that bigotry and fear of otherness will fade into oblivion."

"How's that working out for you so far?" Audrey asks bluntly.

"It's an imperfect system. But I have seen it work. It's real hard to hate people whose life experiences you share."

"What about gay people?" she asks.

"What do you mean?"

"How are same-sex Changers and Statics supposed to have kids?" she asks, thinking it through and calming down a notch as a result.

"Oh, well," I say, a little taken aback, but relieved at a question. "All Changers are kind of postgay and postgender. But as far as how they want to present, the various Changers

Councils arrange for donors and surrogates. It's all thought out, however people want to live their lives."

"I see," Audrey says, at last slumping into my desk chair. *Whew.*

We stop talking for a beat, me eyeing her, reading the signs for imminent disaster. Even stressed and embattled, Audrey is somehow ethereal, hair mussed from bed, cheeks flushed. I wish I could go to her and kiss her and we could get back into bed and lie there for the next hundred years.

"I think you're my Static," I say softly.

She doesn't respond. I can see her eyes are glassy.

"But we're not supposed to think about Static mates until our Cycles are complete," I continue. "Because, I mean, obviously, we change so much, and they don't want us basing our decisions on who our partners might prefer us to be. Or to burden Statics with all our baggage until we are who we are. Also, we're young, so . . ."

"That makes sense," she says.

I approach her slowly; she doesn't back away this time. I reach out to hug her, and she relents.

"But I know you're my One," I whisper into the top of her hair. And I hold her like that, close and tight, the morning sun beaming through the gaps in my curtains.

See? I can slam the brakes at any time.

"I think you may be my One too," she says, but then starts weeping.

"What's wrong?" I ask.

"It's all so much. So confusing. It's just a lot."

"Yeah."

"And now, here you are doing it again, making me be-

lieve in you, in this. I must seem like such a sucker to you."
She pulls back. "You're only coming clean about everything
because you got caught."

I put my head in my hands to cover my face. Feel my
patience slipping. "I told you why: I was protecting you."

"From what?" she asks louder. "If I'm your Static, I'm
your One, then tell me what you're protecting me from."

"I'm afraid to!"

"Why?"

"Because it's ME!"

Audrey's eyes flash with fear. "What do you mean?
How? Are you dangerous?"

"No. I'm not. Mostly. It's a Changer thing." I'm losing
the plot.

"Changers are dangerous?"

I can tell she's scared. Why wouldn't she be? All she
knows about Changers she learned from me, and now I'm
not to be trusted. Everything I've ever said to her could be
a lie. Changers could be a race of serial killers for all she
knows. I could be harvesting her ovaries while she sleeps. I
see her brain clicking, logic fighting with her feelings, dis-
mantling every happy memory, one by one.

"Changers aren't dangerous. It's me. I saw something in
my head," I say.

"If you knew you were dangerous somehow, why would
you come near me? If you have some *thing*, why would you
put me at risk? Is that love to you?"

"Please, Audrey." But I can feel it is too late.

"I need to go," she says curtly. She stands up from the desk.
I move to stop her and she flinches. "Don't come near me."

At that, my brain snaps into some other mode. I see red, a cliché I never understood until I watched blood-colored explosions flash across my line of vision.

"What do YOU know about LOVE?" I spit, unable to stop the words from tumbling out. "You're the one who threw me over the minute Kyle showed up! You were supposed to be waiting for me. But I saw you. The *first* day you met Kyle you wanted him. I didn't see you pining away for Kim."

"Get out of my way!" she screams, trying to exit, but I block the door.

"And what about how you treated Kim during junior year? Was it because I was fat and uncool? Because Chloe didn't approve of me? Were you being such a good person then, Aud? Poor little Audrey. Torn between popularity and basic decency. Is that love to YOU?"

"How can you say all this?" she asks, truly wounded. "I liked Kim."

"Not the way you liked Kyle."

"This is so insane, what are you saying? You ARE Kyle! You're the same freaking person!"

"Yeah, but you didn't *know* that. You're such bullshit, Audrey."

"You know what? I can't, I can't," she says, wheeling around me. "I can't deal with you, I can't deal with this. You're talking nonsense. This is never happening again."

"Wait." I grab her wrist, hard, and she winces, but yanks free.

And our fate is sealed.

I followed her outside.

And it unfolded exactly as it was foreshadowed.

Audrey was starting her car, the window rolled down for the heat.

I ran over, began arguing more through the window.

She screamed. I screamed back.

She reached for the key to crank the ignition. I grabbed her arm.

The car started anyway.

I tried reaching through the steering wheel and around the post to cut the engine.

"I hate you, Kyle!"

And then she hit the accelerator. Sped down the block.

A screech, followed by a loud CRASH I could feel through the pavement, vibrating into my feet, my knees.

Immediate smoke, then flames. A horn nonstop blasting.

I ran toward it.

Audrey's side of the car was impossibly twisted around the front of a massive delivery truck. She was leaning across the horn, the airbag failing to inflate, flames licking her windshield. The driver of the truck wandering around, dazed.

I pried the passenger-side door open. The heat and smell almost unbearable. I put my arms around Audrey's limp body, and the horn stopped. Then I pulled her across the console, and out onto the sidewalk. Then picked her up and laid her on somebody's lawn, far enough away from her car to be sheltered when it blew. Which it did, as I covered her body with mine until the pieces of car stopped falling out of the sky around us.

And then I heard sirens in the distance.

CHANGE 4-DAY 242

I was roused by the last voice you ever want to hear waking you up.

"Dude, you gotta get out of here," Jason said, jerking me vigorously.

At first I didn't remember where I was, but then I heard the sound of Audrey's ventilator, and realized I must've fallen asleep in the chair next to her hospital bed.

"Dude, my dad is going to go ham if he sees you in here," Jason warned.

But it was too late.

Audrey's father came into the room and, as Jason suspected, went "ham" on me and everybody else in there, screaming about how could they let me in here, when Audrey wouldn't have been in an accident if she hadn't snuck off to be with me that night in the first place.

Jason held his father back from coming after me, while the nurse pled, "Please, sir, this is incredibly delicate equipment. You could harm your daughter."

I couldn't believe he was doing this while Audrey was lying there. Who knew how much she was absorbing, and worse, how confusing it must be to hear all these people in her life at odds in the room around her. I didn't want to prolong the drama, so I quickly grabbed my backpack and split before it could get any worse.

"And don't come back!" Audrey's dad hollered after me, while staff whipped heads around toward the ruckus, clearly uncomfortable with this guy shattering the delicate hush of all the sick people with their grieving loved ones gathered around them.

It made me want to turn around and give him some perspective on all of the ways I knew he wasn't able to be there for his daughter over the last four years. But I thought better of it, and went home, where my parents were waiting, begrudgingly accepting my choice to drop-kick my life so I could hold vigil at Audrey's side.

The worst had happened and I was to blame. There was no punishment they or the Council could hand down that I would give a crap about. And they knew it.

CHANGE 4-DAY 244

My nurse ally was on the overnight shift, so she let me sit by Audrey's side again. She said Audrey's vitals improved ever so slightly when I was around. Maybe she was telling me that to make me feel better.

This time I set the alarm on my phone to make sure I was up by the time official visiting hours started.

I don't go to school anymore.

CHANGE 4-DAY 245

This morning they took Audrey off the ventilator.

She can breathe on her own.

Her external wounds are healing.

But she hasn't regained consciousness.

No one knows what will happen if and when she does.

We've been told not to have expectations.

CHANGE 4-DAY 246

Went to see Audrey overnight, as has become my routine.

Without the tube, and through a clear oxygen mask, Audrey looked more like herself. It also helped that a nurse had untaped her eyelids, because they were starting to flutter unconsciously, even open sometimes.

I kissed her on the cheek when we were alone.

One of her fingers moved.

CHANGE 4-DAY 247

Last night I cried in front of Audrey for the first time since she landed in the hospital.

What happened was I finally said, "I'm sorry."

Sorry for chasing her from the house. For saying she didn't love me right. For putting her in the hospital. For wanting what I wanted when I wanted it.

Sorry that I never reported Jason to the police for sexual predation. That I didn't call him on his crime. That I didn't use my power for good. That I did the easy thing instead of the right thing.

Sorry that I'd let myself believe what the culture was reflecting back at me: that I was untouchable. That nothing bad could befall me. That tragedy was for other people. That I deserved whatever I decided I deserved. That this world and everything in it was mine for the taking.

The more I talked, the more I was filled with such relief and gratitude that there was even an Audrey to apologize to, the tears came and came and came. I rested my forehead gently beside her hip until my sobbing finally wound down. The blanket was soaked.

"I'm so, so sorry, Audrey," I wailed.

I felt something on my hair. She was touching me with her hand.

"Kyle," she rasped.

CHANGE 4-DAY 253

Audrey was released from the hospital a few days ago, and while I didn't want to show my face, I had to go to school today to collect the makeup assignments for her. Because of the coma, and massive, soul-destroying guilt, I've missed so many days of classes that Mr. Crowell strong-armed me into his homeroom between periods to give me a talking-to.

"You're in danger of not getting out of here if you miss any more days of school," he said.

"I don't care."

"You may not, but I know a lot of folks who do."

I grunted. "I'm not going to stand by and watch Audrey miss graduation because of this."

"That's admirable, but what about *your* graduation?" he asked.

I shrugged my shoulders. Honestly, how anyone could care about this ritual in the wake of real tragedy, I'll never comprehend.

"How's she doing?" he asked then, relenting from Mr. Hardass.

"Better," I said. "It's slow going, but . . ."

"How are *you* doing? We haven't seen you much since, well, right after it happened."

(Ah yes, when I randomly stopped by the Crowell household ostensibly to "see the new baby," but really to sneak back into Tracy's mirrored box and use the fob to reactivate my Chronicling chip. After my attempted Changer-hack failed, I needed to make sure I was going to be able to escape the hell that had become my Cycle. I didn't want anything sabotaging my Forever Ceremony.)

"I'm fine," I said, not wanting to talk about it. "I'm assuming Tracy has kept you up to speed on everything?"

He nodded his head. "Terrible business."

"Well, I pulled the pin on the grenade."

"Not from what I understand. The predestined vision snafu," he offered.

"Can't say I didn't see it coming," I tried, gallows-humoring it up.

Mr. Crowell seemed genuinely concerned about me. He'd seen how shattered I'd been. *A ghost*, Tracy remarked the last time I saw her. I was such a mess after the accident—dropping fifteen pounds, never sleeping, resembling your basic twitchy dopehead—she didn't even try to guide or educate me, only said, *I can't imagine what you're going through.* I knew I'd put her in the shite again, hooking up with Audrey against direct orders. But maybe the baby had softened Tracy. Or made her so sleep-deprived she had no lectures left to give.

"Well, there's ten days left," Mr. Crowell spelled out. "You need to be here for nine of them to graduate. And finals count."

"Yep. Thank you. I mean it." And I did. Because Mr. Crowell had always been there for me, even when I wasn't. The very definition of a good father.

"Oh, we never got a chance to tell you we settled on a baby name," he said right before I left.

I turned back around. "Oh yeah, what is it?"

"Ethan."

It wasn't until school let out and I was traveling to Audrey's rehab that the impact of Tracy naming her child Ethan washed over me. It made me tear up (which was happening a lot lately, despite how much harder—I can say definitively—it is to cry as Oryon and Kyle, as opposed to Drew and Kim). Tracy is a dark horse. Always busting out the love when I least expect it. I really need to make things right with her before this is all over. For both Ethans' sakes.

I made it across town in twenty minutes. Audrey was in occupational therapy when I knocked on the door of the activities room. She rolled her eyes at me as soon as I walked in, like being asked to put a can of peas on a shelf ten times in a row is the dumbest thing in the world. Which it kind of is—for her. But she's one of the fortunate ones, as evidenced by a quick glance around the unit at the other regulars recovering from far more severe traumatic brain injuries than Audrey.

We sat down at one of the round tables, and I relayed what the teachers said about her assignments. What can be ignored or put off, which are required to get credit. Which teachers are letting her submit alternate work in lieu of sitting for finals. (Which in typical Audrey fashion she probably can and definitely wants to do, though her doctors and parents are strongly suggesting she doesn't, to give her brain and body some more time to recover.)

"How did I get so lucky?" Audrey asks in the middle of a makeup math quiz.

"Trust me, I'm the lucky one," I say.

"God, you're cute. He's really good-looking, right?" she says to her rehab liaison Hillary.

"He's a cutie pie," Hillary responds, used to it by now. "Let's do some strength training, and then you two lovebirds can get out of here."

I watch as Hillary straps Audrey into the leg curl machine on her stomach, and Aud starts pumping away, while reading *Their Eyes Were Watching God.* Our English teacher is letting her submit a paper about swapping traditional gender roles in the book as a final project in place of a final exam. (I can definitely help her with that.)

Everybody keeps saying how lucky she is to have bounced back from such a violent accident, which caused so much trauma to her brain. Her parents have even relented and allowed me to be around. Mostly because the first morning she was conscious, and her dad came in and noticed I was still there, it was Audrey who from her bed shouted, "NO!" loud as she could in her scratchy post-trache voice, when her dad demanded that I leave. Much is forgiven when you've been given a life back. And Audrey is the golden girl of rehab, the patient who will be walking out of here in a week or so, to go on and live an essentially unhindered life, this accident soon to be reduced to one of many bumps in the road.

Which unfortunately can't be said for most of the other folks working equally hard around her.

There's sixteen-year-old Zach on the tilt table, who suffered a right subdural hematoma in a football game; half of his skull was removed in surgery, so there's essentially brain covered with just scalp on one side, and he has to wear a helmet all the time, unless he's strapped into bed with no danger of falling out. His arms are completely numb and limp, he can move his legs slightly and with enormous effort, but can't talk—although his mother insists he understands everything going on around him.

Jaime was a semipro motocross rider who crashed in a race in North Georgia. He's learning the letters of the alphabet all over again with the help of colored magnets on a refrigerator.

Then there's Madison, suspended in a sling between a set of bars over a mat. She was also in a car accident, hit head-on by a drunk driver a few months back. She can walk some, with the help of leg braces and parallel bars. Her speech is slurred, half of her face inert.

Observing these kids fighting to pick up a spoon or say their own names is a constant reminder of how trivial my problems are. Fretting over who I'm going to be in a couple weeks. What a privilege it is even to consider such a thing. To have four healthy lives to choose from, much less one.

All I really care about anymore is that Audrey is okay, and I am doing everything in my power to make sure her life is disrupted as little as possible, now that she has a second chance at it. I'm going to make sure she graduates on time. That she can get out of here and away from her family and go to college like she planned. She'd officially accepted admission to Barnard in New York the day before the accident; I watched her drop the acceptance letter in a mailbox myself.

Audrey moves on to bicep curls while Hillary makes notations about progress on a clipboard. Madison mumbles something loudly from the other side of the room, pivots her head around, and then crooked-smiles at me real big and cute. She insists on writing something on a dry-erase board, won't relent until her nurse agrees, holding the board flat while Madison slowly scribbles against it. The nurse giggles, then brings the board over to show me what the girl has written: *If Audrey dumps you, here's my number.*

"Deal!" I say, flashing a thumbs-up.

"What a sweetheart!" the nurse gushes.

But in reality I don't feel so sweet.

There's a wrinkle, you see. Always a wrinkle with me.

After Audrey came to, the doctor explained that it's unlikely she will ever recall anything from the day of the crash. Nor does she have much long-term memory. Her whole high school experience wiped clean. (Lucky.) Most TBI patients don't remember their accidents, she added. In time, parts of Aud's long-term memory should eventually return, even if all the parts don't always fit together. Which is basically the definition of our lives together—a bunch of parts that make sense when taken alone in segments, but don't necessarily add up when you combine them.

This prognosis was confirmed tonight, when I finally brought Audrey the charm bracelet, which had been sitting on the table next to my bed since she took it off and left it there that tragic day. I was too scared to touch it the whole time she was in the hospital, afraid it would jinx her recovery in some way. I stared at it like a poisonous talisman, remnants of a curse.

But today, with her health on such good footing, I grabbed the bracelet, jamming it in my pocket for later. Audrey and I haven't talked about anything. I mean, we never have to if she doesn't want to. Or if it doesn't come up. The facts lost at sea forever. For the time being, I am content to be what she believes I am: her handsome, devoted boyfriend of many years. And in some ways, the ways that matter, she's right. What good could come of unpacking all that other mess? Especially now.

After rehab, I take Audrey to Pho Sure, the Vietnamese restaurant I first brought her to sophomore year. I put my hand on her back to steady her as we walk in (her gait is evening out, but she has a single arm crutch with a wrist brace because her steps are slower and more unsteady than before).

"This place is great," she says when we reach the table and I pull a chair out for her. "How'd you find it?"

Same question she asked me two years ago. As soon as she sits down and I push her chair in, I lean her crutch up against the wall like I leaned Oryon's crutches up against the wall after Jason and Baron intentionally busted my ankle in football practice. I can't tell if it's time for a "the more things change, the more they say the same" chestnut, or maybe it's more of a "full-circle" moment. Or perhaps "what comes around goes around" is most befitting.

Right after the veggie spring rolls with peanut sauce arrive, I tell Audrey to close her eyes and hold out her palm. She smiles, then complies. After a few seconds of watching her motionless face, I place the bracelet in her palm. "Okay, open," I tell her.

"Oh my god!" she says, picking it up between two fingers, studying all of the charms hooked at various places on the chain: the airplane, drum kit, paddleboat—and the four letters.

After a few seconds of the bracelet dangling in the space between us, she asks, "Are these things from our life together?"

"Kind of," I say.

She examines it even more closely, and it honestly seems like things might be flooding back to her for a second. But then: "What do the D and O stand for?"

"I'll tell you some other time. Do you like it?"

"I love it," she says. "Help me put it on."

CHANGE 4-DAY 255

Tracy texted from outside the house. She needed help getting Ethan inside with all his accoutrements. Stroller, BabyBjörn, diaper bag, breast pump, pacifier on a lanyard, extra clothes in case Ethan craps himself. (God, America sucks sometimes.) When I went out to the curb, she just held Ethan in front of me and said, "Here, take this."

I had never held a baby. Tracy wasn't about caring. Surveying him dangling in the air between us, I got spooked that I was going to drop him or break him or somehow smush the soft part in the back of his head that everybody seems paranoid about around babies. It's crazy to be handed a whole life like that.

You got this, Kyle; it's only a little baby, I thought to myself, and reached my hands out, hooking them under his tiny armpits, and floated him toward me, carefully transitioning him into the cradle of my arms with his neck being supported by a bicep. He was so tiny and delicate. But kind of cute, now that I was really taking a good peep at him.

"Let's get him out of the sun, I forgot to bring a hat," Tracy said, various quilted, flower-patterned bags swinging off her body while she yanked the car seat out of the car and kicked the door closed behind her in one deft motion.

I walked gingerly into the house with baby Ethan, Mom more than happy to grab him the minute we passed over the threshold. I didn't really want to give him up, but Tracy and I needed to talk. I knew what was in one of those flowered bags: my Chronicles from the last four years. My entire soap opera of high school life conveniently bound in four thick notebooks.

"Are you going to be okay?" Tracy asks Mom, who's cooing into Ethan's face.

"Of course we're okay. Aren't we okay?" Mom goo-goo-ga-gas.

In my room Tracy slides out the notebooks and drops them on my desk with a thud. "I couldn't help but notice Y-4 was a little thinner than the other three," she says. "Ahem."

"Yeah, I meant to mention that. I need to come clean about something."

"Oh, I already know," Tracy says.

"You read them?"

"No, we don't read them! These are for you guys alone. Why does everyone assume we read them? Like I have no life of my own?" she mutters, sitting down. "There was a note on file that Chronicling had gone dark for about four months, and I did the math."

"I'm sorry, I was desperate."

"I don't love you snooping through my things."

I flood with shame. "I'm sorry."

"It's okay," she says. "Teachable moment, no?"

"Beyond."

"That's good to hear. The truth is, there was nothing I could've told you that would've changed what happened. That vision was going to play out, period. No matter what you thought you could do about it. I didn't know how to tell you that. It's simply something you kind of have to learn for yourself. All of us do."

I guess. But I'll forever feel horrified by my role in what Audrey went through. I pick up the Y-4 notebook and rub a finger over the Changers emblem embossed on the cover.

"So, this is going to be quite the journey, reflecting back," Tracy says. "I never thought we'd get here, and yet we are. It feels like it happened so fast. I guess all parents says that. You know, you were my first."

"Your first Changer?" I ask.

"Yes. But that's not what I mean, silly billy. My first kid. That's how it feels anyhow."

I'm not prepared for the emotion welling in my chest and throat, so I divert my attention, crack the Y-4 notebook and look through mindlessly, the air fanning up on my face from the heavy pages flipping by. My thumb stops on the last page with writing, where, HOLY SHIT, *these words I'm thinking and Chronicling right here are being recorded and appearing before my eyes.*

Wow. That is some crazy magic shizz.

"I guess I've got a lot of processing to do. I feel so pressed for time. How am I supposed to digest all of these in two weeks?" I drop the open notebook on top of the other three.

"Once you get started, it'll fly by. It's like you're watching the movie of your life," Tracy says.

"A horror film, no doubt."

"Hardly," she says. "You should hear the stories I hear at Changers Central. Some real doozies. But anyway, do you have any hunch who you're going to declare?"

I grimace. "I really don't."

It's unnerving not knowing who you're going to be in a couple weeks' time. Although, as I learned from Audrey's accident, none of us really know. Life changes in an instant. Whether you're preparing for it or not.

"You'll make the right choice for you," Tracy says.

"You already knew by now, right? You knew the minute you woke up as Tracy."

"I did. But that doesn't mean I didn't think about my other options."

"And you still picked Tracy?" I tease.

"You're not too big to punish, Kyle. Don't make me snatch you bald-headed."

I feel my heart break a tad, thinking about losing Tracy as my Touchstone, her attention needed at home, with the baby. I took her for granted most of the time. She never bailed on my delinquent butt. Never wavered. Little Ethan doesn't know how lucky he is.

"Here's the thing: there are no redundant pieces of the universe," she chirps. "Think of it like a giant machine that keeps life happening. Every single part of that machine plays a role in the process, every piece fits somewhere and does its job. Some are pumps, some are belts, some are nuts or bolts that hold everything together. Some are the fuel that runs through the system to make all those pieces function. You have four different parts you've played in the bigger picture at different times, all of them contributing something vital. You need to choose which part you felt most comfortable playing. Which job suited you best, what part you can see yourself playing for the rest of your life."

"No biggie," I say, walloped anew by the enormity of the decision before me.

"I have a gift for you." She roots around in her bag and presents a box wrapped in green (gender neutral!) paper. "Open it up!"

I do. It's a mug.

"What other people think of me is none of my business," I read off the side of the ceramic.

"Word!" Tracy shouts, making a fist to bump mine. "Am I right?"

We bump fists the way only two white people can.

"Thank you. I'm sorry I was a jerk so much of the time," I say.

"You gave me these wrinkles, child." She points at her forehead. "But I'm not even a little worried about you doing the right thing. You know why?"

"No."

"Because there is no right thing. There's just the thing itself."

(If I had to bet, she saw that on a mug too.)

CHANGE 4-DAY 259

Dad came home in a mood.

He'd been at Changers Central all afternoon, getting indoctrinated—I mean, brought up to speed at the annual State of the Changers Union Council retreat. When he returned, he stormed through the kitchen yelling about where was his iPad, and why was the house always such a sty.

Mom corralled him into the bedroom and after thirty minutes of angry whispering, Dad went back to the kitchen, poured himself a tumbler of Scotch, and asked me to sit down with him. Apparently, we needed to talk.

I was sure it was about Audrey, or about me being a crap Changer, or some other more mundane way I was letting him and our family down. But when I joined him at the table, I could tell from his expression that he was less angry than really, really forlorn.

"Take a seat, son," he began. "I have something you need to hear."

Oh boy.

"In my debriefing today, I was made privy to some information. When I joined the Council, I took an oath to keep any and all information private. What I am about to do will break that oath, and will likely mean my immediate dismissal from the Council leadership."

"But Dad, you worked for that position for years," I said.

He nodded and swallowed a gulp of Scotch. "After consulting with your mother, I have made the determination that I don't give a shit."

Then he laid it on me: RaChas HQ was not burned down by the Abiders, and it wasn't a random accident; the fire was set by the Council. They'd discovered that Benedict was outing every Changer he knew, posting their photos and particulars on his blog, and the Council decided the only way to stop him was to destroy his resources and frighten him out of town.

Freaking Benedict.

"When I heard," Dad said, "my first thought was that you lived there once. You could have been in that building. My kid could have died."

"Nobody died, Dad."

"That's not the point. I've strayed so far from who I thought I was. These past few years, all I could see was the mission, the chance for you to be braver, better than I was. I pressured you to make up for my failings. That's why I've embraced Kyle so much. Because Kyle is, well, Kyle. He'd be an incredible Changer soldier. Or so I imagined."

He took another long drink.

"It's ironic. In my obsession to elevate Changerkind, I lost sight of what being a Changer actually means. How every V holds advantages and liabilities. How every V teaches the world something valuable. How little the outside shell means in the end."

I swallowed a small swig then too.

"I'm sorry, Kyle. I'm sorry, Kim. Oryon. Drew. I'm so sorry. I don't know how I could have lost my way." Dad threw his head on the table, folded his arms over the top. He was getting a little drunk, of course. But I chose to believe he meant what he said nonetheless.

"We all lose our way, Dad," I said, unsure if I should touch him. "That's why we have a family. To show us the way home." I patted him a couple times on the back.

He lifted his head, shot me a bleary eye. "You know you and Mom are always home to me, right?"

CHANGE 4-DAY 261

Reading these Chronicles induces that same gut punch you get when you hear your own recorded voice for the first time. Except the Chronicles make you a million times more uncomfortable and self-conscious. Revisiting every boneheaded decision I've made in the last four years. Seeing my wants and needs splashed all over the page like so much teenage ooze.

I've spent the last six days with these journals, and I'm only up to the day before I became Kim. I'm trying to get them read before I need to turn the minimum of attention to finals, which start in two days.

It dawns on me that I might benefit from some external perspective. No *Changers Bible* rule against that. So I head out to the living room, where Andy's sitting cross-legged in the middle of his pullout bed, split-open books and papers spread out in a circle around him.

"Hey, man, what are you up to?" I ask.

"What does it look like I'm up to? Trying not to fail chemistry and having to repeat a third junior year. What about you?"

"Not studying. Got this Forever Ceremony coming up after graduation," I say, and plop on the love seat across from him. He's a tad irked that I'm taking time away from his cramming. Which I am. But I need a friend. One who's been there since the beginning, even if he wasn't here for all of the in-between.

"Yeah, your mom told me a little about that. That is some sci-fi realness, dude."

"I'm paralyzed," I say. "I mean, there's this whole part of me that wants to stay like this, because then I won't have to go through a whole change again, and it's not like this is the worst person to be in the world."

"What about Audrey?" he asks, putting down his pencil.

"Yeah, that's the other part," I admit. "A big part."

"What are you gonna do about her?"

"I don't know," I say, rubbing my eyes really hard with my knuckles. When I stop, there are four blurry Andys in front of me. "I really love her, but if I don't pick Kyle, then I can't be with her. Because she doesn't remember any of my other V's."

"Quite a pickle," Andy says.

"I'm serious, it's about to kill me."

"I get how serious it is. I've been ghosted by a Changer before, remember?"

"I think Audrey's my One," I say, the only time I've spoken it aloud to anybody but her. "But what if Kyle isn't who I'm supposed to be?"

Andy nods his head quietly, pondering.

"Do I seem like Kyle to you?" I ask him.

"What does that mean?"

"Like, does this person seem like *me*?" I'm not even really sure what I'm asking.

"I guess," he says.

"So not really?"

He thinks about it for a few seconds while I pet Snoopy, who'd waggled over for a scratch. "I guess if I'm honest, you still seem like Ethan to me, or at least that's how I think of you."

"Okay."

He goes on, "But you're Ethan who's lived through a lot over the last four years, regardless of who you lived those years as. Does that make any sense?"

"So I'm aging like a president."

He starts laughing. "It almost doesn't matter who you pick for your exterior, because you're still the same person I've always known . . . a loser." Andy is amused as hell at himself.

"Sick burn," I say flatly. "Really. The sickest."

"One serious question, though, if I may," Andy adds, as I get up to head back to my room. "Was Drew hot? Like someone I'd want to smash? Because if so, definitely pick one of the other three."

I hurl a pillow at him, then go back to the journals to take a little trip down Kim Cruz lane.

CHANGE 4-DAY 268

It didn't rain on graduation like they were calling for. In fact, it was clear skies for miles.

Mom and Dad were seated eleven rows back from the stage, Andy next to Dad, and Tracy next to Mom, the two of them passing baby Ethan (in a ginormous sun hat) back and forth between them every time he fussed. Mr. Crowell was up on the dais, there to hand out the humanities awards.

I'm seated with the S row of grads donned in plain blue caps and gowns, no extra accoutrements. Audrey is, of course, with Michelle in the crushing-it-in-high-school section in the front rows, for students graduating with a 3.9–4.0 GPA. Which means they have fancy gold sashes around their necks and over their gowns, like the intellectual elites they are.

Luckily, I'm not all alone back here, as Kris is in the T section, which ended up being one row and two seats behind me. He (or I should say *she* now) has a striped maxi-dress on under her gown, barely peeking out from the hem. And chunky Fluevog wedges that look like something a stripper on Venus might wear.

"*I'm coming out, I want the world to know, got to let it show,*" Kris whisper-sings Diana Ross from behind me.

"Shhh," the kid next to her hisses.

"*Really?*" I say, pulling a tough-guy face at the kid—

me the star quarterback with a full ride to play at a D-1 school—and he instantly snaps back to minding his own business, sweating there in his too-tight and way-too-wide necktie.

As valedictorian, Michelle is called up to speak. She nails it. Hits all the notes: social justice, responsibility to our environment, hope for the future. Her moms go nuts when she crumples up her speech and grins at the audience with that crooked, adorable, pursed-lip smirk that she works.

The academic awards are announced after that (Michelle collects two), and then us plebes receive our diplomas, marching one by one in alphabetical order like every high school graduation everywhere ever, as the principal repeatedly leans into the mic and reminds everybody not to yell out or clap after each graduate, or we'll be here all day.

Which it already feels like we have, what with the sun and a last name that begins with S. But then I see Audrey's row released, her inching her way up the stairs, her little gold sash flapping in the breeze behind her. She's still using the wrist-support cane for her left side, and as soon as her name is called, the crowd erupts like she has just risen from the dead.

My heart swells with pride. Admiration. She made it. She graduated. Screw you, coma! I check back on Kris over my shoulder. Her eyes are brimming, and she's manically fanning them, trying to prevent her lashes from sailing away.

Then I look at my mom and dad, and Tracy, who forms a Taylor Swift heart with her hands when she catches my eye. I'll bet she's happy I'm her first and last Changer, so she won't have to sit through another interminable high school graduation ceremony until it's Ethan's turn (in whatever V he gets for his senior year).

We sit and wait for what seems like another decade, and then my row is finally asked to approach the stage. My walk happens in a flash. As in, there's all this nervous anticipation, hours of baking in the sun, and poof! I find myself accepting my diploma with my left hand, and shaking hands with the row of administrators and teachers with my right—and then it's over. Just like that.

When I reach the edge of the stage, Mr. Crowell stands awkwardly and pulls me into a hug, and the audience erupts with some audible "Awws" and claps.

"I'm so proud of everything you've accomplished," he whispers during the embrace. When he lets go, I see his hands are trembling.

I'm on my way back to my seat when Kris goes up to the stage; the only reason I realize she's headed up is because of the uncomfortable titters and giggles in the crowd, especially among students, as though there's been a disturbance in the gender force field.

I stop in time to see her sashay up those stairs and work that runway, like it's grad-RU-ation day (shout out to Mama RuPaul). Never one to take the easy route, Kris decided she wanted to start socially transitioning before graduation. Her folks refused to attend if she insisted on wearing that dress, thinking Kris would back down. Which was the dumbest bet in the history of dumb.

After the ceremony wraps, I'm strolling to the field to meet my family, but Coach Tyler intercepts and congratulates me. He doesn't seem to want to stop pumping my hand, but then my mom and dad come up, with Andy and Tracy in tow, so Coach gives me a nod and says, "Good luck next year. We'll be watching you," then heads off to find his other graduating players.

Mom and Dad are already full-snot crying. *Tracy* is full-snot crying. Ethan is crying because it's so goddamn hot out here and he hates that giant hat. Andy is not crying. Good golly gumdrops for that. (Lord only knows what tomorrow at the Forever Ceremony is going to be like with this sensitive lot.)

I see Audrey making her way toward me with the hitch in her step, her family staying a few paces behind. I run to her, pick her up like she's the new girl on *Bachelor in Paradise*. We kiss right there in front of everybody—her family, my family, and the whole graduating class—and then I let her slide down my body and make sure she's steady on her feet before I let go.

"Well, we did it!" I say.

"I couldn't have done it without you," she says.

"Are you kidding me? Wasn't me who pulled a 3.95 GPA."

Kris comes up to us squealing, kisses Audrey, then me.

"Hang with us," I say, knowing Kris doesn't have any family to support her today.

"Third wheel as ever," she laments.

"Well, you look beautiful," I tell her.

"Well, well, what have we here?" And . . . it's Jason. Slithering up right on cue.

"Jason, you remember my friend Kris," Audrey says firmly, praying he'll act right for once in his redneck life.

Kris extends her hand. "Charmed, I'm sure."

"Don't touch me, freak show," Jason snaps.

"What's your problem, man?" I say, stepping to him in my flowing gown.

"My problem is, if you're a Y, you're a guy. Pretty simple."

"Shut up, Jason," Audrey says.

"Ex-queer me?" he snipes.

At that, I crowd even closer to him, so tight he can feel my breath. "I've been meaning to tell you this for a long time," I start then, low and quiet so only he can hear. "I don't know if you actually are an Abider, or you just play one on weekends. Either way, I don't care. Because you and your gang of phobic assholes? You're all suckers. You're dim and you're ignorant and you can't even sense yourself sliding into an oblivion where your every thought and opinion is irrelevant, and you along with it. No matter how much hate you spew or how many people you shame with your backward, primordial, lizard-brain theories, in a few years, maybe less, you won't matter at all. That train, my friend, has already left the station."

Jason tries to step back, but I grab his elbow, squeeze it tourniquet-tight.

"Oh, and one more thing. I see you, Jason. And for the rest of your sad life on this planet, I will be watching you. Know that. If you so much as take a single baby step out of line, I will expose you to every college football recruiter, every potential employer, everyone you even think you care about—as a sexual predator, a racist, a liar, an abusive thug. I will set your life on fire and I will warm my hands on the flame. Hear me?"

Jason just stands there dumbfounded, so Kris, Audrey, and I all turn and sashay away—and I mean that literally. We wiggle our butts and werk that imaginary catwalk, and I can just imagine Jason's bug eyes popping out of their sockets and bouncing into the grass.

CHANGE 4-DAY 268, PART TWO

I finished reading all my Chronicles. *Up to this place right here, where these words are being recorded as I watch on the last empty pages.* (That'll never not be astonishing.)

In less than twenty-four hours I will be declaring my Mono for the whole universe to see, from here on out. How many times have I longed for this control? Whined and moaned, all *Why can't I be in charge of my own fortune?*

And now that I have it? No thank you, sir. Swipe. Left.

The no-brainer choice is Kyle, man of everyone's dreams. My dad would be stoked (even if he's singing a more evolved tune these days). Life would be easy. And, of course, there's Audrey. Who only knows Kyle. And who adores him.

Facetime buzzes; it's Elyse.

"Happy night before Halloween!" she yells as soon as I connect. She's flashing two cheesy thumbs-up as the picture snaps into view.

"Hey."

"Dang, you seem less than psyched. What you got cooking over there? Making your pro and con lists? I know you dig those decision charts."

"They aren't working," I moan.

"They never work. How don't people realize that?"

I catch my face in the square above Elyse's. I look tired. "How does anyone do this?"

"I threw a dart at a wall," she says.

"Not helping."

"Listen, it's tough. I won't lie. But the good news is that by this time tomorrow, it'll all be over. ALL of it! And you'll get to settle into whatever horribly bad choice you made that will haunt you forever for the rest of time."

I snort begrudgingly. "Well, thanks for calling, E. You've been a tremendous help."

"I'll see you tomorrow, boo bear. Been a long road. But the fun is just getting started. Trust me," she says, throwing up deuces. "Peace out!"

I close my laptop and walk into the TV room, where Mom's watching that unbelievably dull British countryside real estate show that's like her crack.

"Do you have a minute?"

"Of course I do," she says, clicking off the TV. "Everything okay?"

"Yeah." I plop down on the couch next to her. "No, not really."

"Tomorrow," she says, in that perfect tone that lets you know she cares, but not too much. (She's good at what she does.)

"It's a big decision."

"I don't envy you it," she says, brushing a lint ball off my T-shirt sleeve.

"Can I ask you something? You have to be honest."

"Always."

"Which me did you like best?"

She takes a deep breath. "That's a tough one."

"Truthfully."

"Truthfully? It doesn't matter who I like best. It matters who you like best, right?"

"Come on," I say. "Not a therapist or mom answer. A real answer, like adult to almost-adult."

"Petunia, I can't answer that sort of question," she says. "You're my kid. All of you are my kid. And I love you all the same—because you are the same."

Danke for *nada*.

I'm not sure what I was expecting. I guess some straight-forward answer: *I liked Oryon best! Pick Oryon!* Somewhere, I still want someone to tell me what to do. Which isn't going to happen, at least not with Mom.

"Have you ever tried to change who you were so that somebody would love you?" I ask then.

"You've been a girl twice—you tell me," she says, ending with one of those high-pitched laughs that happen when you realize how effed society is and how if you don't laugh, you'll explode with impotent rage.

"Yeah," I say. "I guess."

"But to answer your question, yes, I have. And it never works out, because whatever you think you need to be for someone, it's never what they really want. You can't reverse-engineer a relationship, so why even try?"

"Yeah, I guess I know what you mean," I say.

"In my opinion, I'd suggest you decide which you *you* love the most. And once you do, the right partner will find you and love that you. But you can't do that if you're worried about what someone else might want you to be."

At that, we hear Andy get home from working a dinner shift. He pops his head into the living room. "Oh, sorry, I didn't mean to interrupt."

"It's okay, we were just finishing up," I say, then lean over and hug Mom. "Thanks."

"I love you. You're a thoroughly lovely human being, and I'm honored to know you."

I smile. "I love you too."

Back in my room, I dig out the container of Nana's things I'd been too emo to sort through before. Inside are some hankies that smell like her floral perfume, some petite vintage flower vases, an apron printed with the words *This ain't your ordinary housewife*, and more crackled black-and-white photographs fraying at the edges. Pictures of Nana posing over the decades—wow, women spent a lot of time on their hair back then. There is also a stack of more modern pictures from the seventies, the colors yellowed and oranged, Nana wearing a pantsuit with a turtle pattern, matching shorts and halter top in another loud pattern, cha cha heels. Nana was fly. And happy, if these photos are any indication, which in this case unlike so many others, I believe they are.

Seeing Nana again reminds me of the letter she wrote me right before she died. I root around in my closet, find my memory box, the note resting there right on top as if somewhere, she sensed I'd need to read it.

Sweet Angel,

I don't know how much time I have left here with you. I really wanted to see you through your Cycles and to be there at your Forever Ceremony, but it's looking

like that isn't going to be possible. I can feel the days slipping away and while I don't love it, there is nothing to
be done, so I may as well enjoy what I can while I'm still
here.

With or without me, I know you are going to find
your way and make the right decision. You are an incredibly special person, and I'm proud to have known
you through a handful of your lives. I could not have
asked for more from a grandchild.

The reason I'm writing you this letter is because I
wanted to share something important with you. Your
father didn't want me to tell you, but I'm too old for stat-
utes and protocol, and besides, I am still his mother and
he is not in charge, much as he'd like to think he is.

What I hope to do is offer you some comfort. Which
is more important than rules any day. I couldn't help
but notice how sad you've been since your friend Chase
passed. It was a terrible thing that happened, and I can
see you tearing yourself up with guilt. That, however, is a
useless emotion, a giant waste of time and energy. Guilt
serves no one and changes nothing. If you don't take my
word for it, I'm confident you'll discover that on your
own someday.

Guilt is especially useless in your case, because your
friend Chase isn't truly gone forever.

I suppose they don't want you to know this because
it might change how you act during your Cycle, or influence your decision about your Mono, but in actuality
there is a system, a method to all this madness.

Your Chase was a recycled version of many other

Chases throughout the centuries. If you take a look at the enclosed photo, you will see that I was the Chase V for a year during my Cycle. And when I didn't choose Chase as my Mono, he was released back into the universe, free to be inhabited by a new Changer just beginning his or her Cycle at some point after me.

Which means that Chase, as an identity, will return. That identity will go on and on, until somebody selects it as their Mono, and completes a lifetime as that V.

I'm sure this is confusing, my love. And more than a little unnerving. I'm still debating whether I should tell you even as I'm sitting here writing. But it's no accident you felt so drawn to this boy, and likely no accident that he protected you the way he did. And it is no wonder you feel his loss so keenly. But you don't have to. Chase will live on. Somewhere. Somehow.

And one day, eventually, we will all know what it's like to be somebody else. To live as another, feel their pain, their joy, make their mistakes, celebrate their triumphs. It really is a gift we've been given to see and experience so much. A gift we must share. Because it does matter, Kim.

What you do matters.

Imagine how different the world is going to be once we reach that place. When there is no difference left to fear. No outsiders. No "other."

I'm not afraid of leaving because I have so much hope for that future—your future.

So, I'll leave you to it, Angel.

I wiped a tear, folded the letter, and laid it gently back in the box, Nana's counsel echoing in my ears along with all the rest . . .

The fun is just getting started.

Because there is no right thing. There's just the thing itself.

You need to decide which you you love the most.

What other people think of me is none of my business.

My V's swirled together in my head like those spiral art kits I used to do in kindergarten. You drop the paint on the spinning wheel and it fans out, takes over the whole paper. Use too much paint and the sheet goes completely gray.

I closed the box, returned it to its spot in the closet, putting the past away.

My future is starting tomorrow.

And I know what I need to do.

CHANGE 4-DAY 269

I texted Audrey to meet me at the river first thing this morning, before my folks and I had to leave for the Forever Ceremony at Changers Central.

Our river.

She pulls up in her mother's sedan a few minutes after I arrive, parking next to me.

"Hey, sailor," she says through the window. "You looking for a good time?"

"Why yes, ma'am. Any idea where I can find one?"

"About twelve miles down the road at the Beaver Hut," she says, rolling up the window and cracking herself up.

I come around to her door, help her out of the car. She'd tied a black-and-white *Happy Graduation!* ribbon around her cane.

"Want to find a bench by the water?" I ask.

"Long as it's in within hobbling distance," she says.

And off we go. The sun has freshly risen, and the frogs are already awake and singing, filling the warm air with their delirious music. We move at Audrey's pace, slow and cautious, so different from before when we would scramble and race ahead like puppies freed from a pen. You take so much for granted in this world, I'm thinking as we make our way to a free bench between the packs of runners and bikers. Even something as simple as jumping a stone.

"How's this?" I ask, brushing a bench clean with my handkerchief, then folding it back into my pants pocket.

"You always were a gentleman."

"*Were?*"

Audrey pats the bench for me to sit beside her. "Let me make this easy for you. We should break up."

I'm gobsmacked. "What makes you think that's what's happening?"

"Isn't it?" Audrey smiles warmly, no hint of anger.

"I don't want to," I say, my voice cracking.

"But?"

I start to turn my body from hers, though she won't let me. She grabs my hands, both of them, holds them tight on her lap.

"It's okay, I understand," she whispers.

She doesn't, of course. Or maybe she does. Audrey has always been so ahead of me, aware of my desires and fears before I've had the wherewithal to articulate them.

"We're both headed to college," she begins. "We'll be far away from each other. Leading separate lives. You'll be throwing footballs at meatheads; I'll be sitting around talking about intersectional feminist theory. Our paths diverging."

"I love you, Audrey."

"I love you too. So much."

It feels like I am ripping out my heart and tossing it down five sets of stairs.

It feels like death.

"If only this were a different time, a different world," I try, just in case there's a sliver of doubt in that beautiful brain of Audrey's, the one I'm so happy has pretty much completely returned to its rightful owner.

"But it isn't," she says softly. "This is our now. We can't make that different. And we shouldn't try to."

I want to kiss her, but I fear I won't survive it.

"I wish I hadn't lost so many memories of us," she says then, teary for the first time in the conversation. "But I know they are in my brain somewhere, waiting to come out. Maybe that's a good thing. They'll be unexpected gifts, sweet surprises, reminders of you when I need them most."

"You were the beginning of my everything, Audrey. I want you to know . . ." But I can't finish.

Because I know what has to happen. To become who I am meant to be, I need to cleave myself from the person who makes me feel most like myself. I need to stand alone.

It just never occurred to me that the same would be true for Audrey.

"If almost dying has taught me anything, it's that this moment is the only moment that counts," she says.

At that, Audrey rises, takes her cane, steadies herself, then leans into me, our lips touching soft as moth wings.

As she does this, I have a vision. Not a fatalistic Changers one. But one from *my* future. I'm in a field of yellow flowers, the sun bright above me. I am laughing. Dogs romping at my feet. I am not alone. I can feel someone there who knows me like she does. And I am happy.

"I'm going to go, and you're going to stay here and watch me," she says, straightening, then pulling away. "But you better stay in touch. Don't you forget about me."

"I'm not the one with the questionable memory," I say.

"Ha ha! Dummy," she laughs.

And then I watch as the woman I've loved for four years slowly, haltingly fades from my sight.

CHANGE 4-DAY 269, PART TWO

This is it.

Time to declare who I am and will be from here on out.

Will the real me please stand up?

Mom and Dad are here in the audience. Tracy and Mr. Crowell, with baby Ethan too. Elyse. (Not Andy; no Statics who aren't in Changers families are allowed at Forever Ceremonies.)

Videos play, members of the Council speak, and it is much like Destiny/Elyse's ceremony I witnessed a year ago. Turner the Lives Coach comes onstage out of the darkness, robes billowing, pacing in the spotlight while speaking into his little flesh-colored headset: "In the many we are one!"

Normally I'd laugh at his cult-babble. But today it lands somewhere else, the full meaning of those words washing over me, and it is the most freeing sensation I have ever experienced. To know that everything before was part of this moment right here. And it's okay to let it all go.

Every touchdown.

Every kiss.

Every drumbeat.

Every fight.

Every choice.

Every death, big and small.

They all brought me here, integral parts of the machine Tracy talked about. The machine that got me where I am about to go.

The lights dim, Mom squeezes my arm, and I am called up, the spotlight following me all the way as I walk from my seat to the podium.

"I know an alternate world is possible because I am a part of it," I say, as I begin my prepared speech, sharing in the simplest terms I can manage about how it felt to revisit my four choices, to reflect on my growth, to see starkly how much growing I still have to do. "And after all is said and done, I am moving ahead in the V where I felt, not so much myself, but the best version of myself." I'm fighting back tears. "I am picking the person I was when I woke up to what life could be. The person whose story I want to finish."

Right then, all of my V's flash up on the screen behind me (and I can see them on the smaller screen hidden in the podium before me). First Drew, then Oryon, Kim, and finally Kyle. I stare at them together in a tight little grid. It's almost as if they're in conversation with one another. (Or in a really hip band.)

I push the first button, and Kyle disappears from the screens.

I can hear a tight gasp from a woman somewhere in the front rows, even if I can't completely see her face.

Bye, Kyle.

And then there were three.

I press another button.

Then another.

And the auditorium fades to black.

And I turn around to face the crowd.

FOREVER

MONO-DAY 92

Where is the freaking coffee shop?

The map on the phone says it should be on this block, and I've searched and searched, but I can't seem to spot it in this crushing sea of humanity streaming up and down both sides of Broadway. This glorious, diverse, epic, heaving, miraculous sea of humanity that is New York City, my new home for the next four years (after swinging admittance to Columbia with the help of the Changers Council).

"Ouch!" Some guy has just run over my shoe with his bike tire.

"Watch where you're going, loser!" the biker shouts over his shoulder.

Ah yes, New York. Where the streets are lined with simmering hostility.

It kind of feels good to be back in Ethan's birth state, embarking on the next big thing. *College, yo!*

Now, my first class: "Intro to Film and Media Studies" in the Dodge building. I flip open the handy laminated campus map they gave us at orientation and locate the building, right on the northeast corner of Broadway and 116th. Easy. I have twelve minutes to get to class. Enough time for a quick coffee—if I can find one.

I squint down the block, ducking around people as they filter around me.

Bingo! I can just make out the ubiquitous green Starbucks logo through the trees in the median, underneath construction scaffolding, and beside an eminently ancient church, so I run across the street with the walk signal and dip inside.

Shit. There's a line, but it seems to be moving fast, so I place my order, pay, and step aside to wait.

Come on, folks. Let's get these orders rolling. My future is now.

"Soy latte?" the bearded barista shouts over the din.

I peek over to see who's picking up the familiar (yet also completely ordinary) order . . .

And there she is.

Wait, it's her, right?

Or do I just *want* it to be her?

The girl's hair looks a little longer, her frame a bit thicker, and there's no cane hanging from her wrist . . .

But it's AUDREY. My Audrey.

And now she's headed to the condiment bar to plunk the usual two sugars into her cup.

The barista calls my name, so I scoop up my iced coffee, pop off the cap, and rush over before Audrey can finish stirring and slip out the door. When I sidle up to the bar, nervous, I accidentally bump her arm, and a little coffee splashes on her sleeve.

"Oh my god, I'm so sorry," I say, grabbing a few square napkins to clean up.

"It's no big deal, really," Audrey laughs. Not a tinge of annoyance in her voice.

"Cute top," I say, blotting her arm with the paper napkin. Heart pounding.

"It's mad chaos in here," she says, seeming a little jittery too. "Like they're actually shilling good coffee or something."

We laugh. Eyes lock. And we stay that way, speechless, for far longer than any two complete strangers would usually hold one another's gaze.

"First day?" Audrey asks finally.

"Uh, yeah," I stammer. "Columbia. You?"

"Across the street, Barnard."

I know.

"Your face is familiar," Audrey says, shifting her weight from one foot to the other. "Have we met?"

Before I can say anything, she hoists her coffee cup to eye level, points at the writing: *Audrie.* "As you can see, I'm Audrey. Only it's Audrey with an E-Y."

"Pleased to meet you, Audrey with an E-Y," I say.

"And you are . . . ?" she asks, while simultaneously reaching over and twisting my cup around so she can read the name scribbled messily on the side.

Our fingers touch around the backside of the cup.

It feels something like the sun.

She reads from the cup.

"It's really nice to meet you," she pauses, "Drew."

THE BEGINNING

ABRIDGED GLOSSARY OF TERMS
(*EXCERPTED FROM* THE CHANGERS BIBLE)

ABIDER. A non-Changer (see *Static*, below) belonging to an underground syndicate of anti-Changers, whose ultimate goal is the extermination of the Changer race. The Abider philosophy is characterized by a steadfast desire for genetic purity, for human blood to remain unmingled with Changer blood. Abider leaders operate by instilling fear in humans, for when people fear one another, they are easier to control. Abiders sometimes have an identifying tattoo depicting an ancient symbol of a Roman numeral I (*Figure 1*), the emblem symbolizing homogeneity and the single identity Abiders desire each human to inhabit.

FIG. 1. ABIDERS EMBLEM

CHANGER. A member of an ancient race of humans imbued with the gift of changing into a different person four times between the ages of approximately fourteen and eighteen. (In more modern times, one change occurs at the commencement of each of the four years of high school; see *Cycle*, below.) Changers may not reveal themselves to non-Changers (see *Static*, below). After living as all four versions of themselves (see *V*, below), Changers must choose one version in which to live out the rest of their lives (see *Mono*, below). Changer doctrine holds that the Changer race is the last hope for the human race on the whole to reverse the moral devolution that has overcome it. Changers believe more Changers equals more empathy on Planet Earth. And that only through empathy will the human race survive. After their Cycles (see *Cycle*, below), Changers eventually partner with Statics. When approved by the Council (see *Changers Council*, below), Changer-Static unions produce a single Changer offspring.

CHANGERS COUNCIL. The official Changer authority. The Changers Council is divided into regional units spread out across the globe. Each Council is responsible for all basic decisions regarding the population of Changers in its specific region.

CHANGERS EMBLEM. A variation on Leonardo da Vinci's *Vitruvian Man* drawing, dating to approximately 1490 CE (*Figure 2*). The Changers emblem contains four bodies superimposed in motion, instead of two (as portrayed in da Vinci's composition), and appears to the eye as both four bodies and one body at the same time—though all sharing one head and heart. An emblem of the Changers mantra: *In the many, we are one.*

FIG. 2. CHANGERS EMBLEM

CHANGERS MIXER. Required events for all Changers to attend, during each of the four years of high school. Council rules and regulations are emphasized at mixers (see *Changers Council,* above). Mixers sometimes require classwork and formal discussions, but they are primarily designed to offer more informal camaraderie and problem-solving techniques, both of which help Changers address some of the difficulties that frequently arise during their Cycles (see *Cycle,* below).

CYCLE. The four-year period of different iterations, or versions (see *V,* below), that a Changer goes through between the approximate ages of fourteen and eighteen. One V per each of the four years of high school, in modern times.

FEINTS. The story a Changer family tells the non-Changers (see *Static,* below) in their lives, to explain each V's (see *V,* below) absence during the following year of school. The specific details for feints are provided by the Council (see *Changers Council,* above), unless a Changer and her/his parents submit a formal request for an alternative feint, which is necessary under certain circumstances (i.e., when Statics are especially integrated into a particular V's life, or when a particular feint will better protect the identity of the Changer and her/his family).

FOREVER CEREMONY. Regional "graduation" events held on the day after high school graduation for every Changer within a designated region. A joyous though private (from Statics—except parental Statics; see *Static,* below) occasion, as each year of ceremonies initiates more and more Changers to migrate into the world and eventually find a Static mate, with whom they will start a family and raise Changer offspring of their own. At the Forever Ceremony Year 4, Changers are introduced one by one, and each speaks a little about each of her/his V's (see *V*, below) before declaring in front of both the Council (see *Changers Council*, above) and their community whom they will live as for the rest of their lives (see *Mono*, below).

MONO. A Changer's "forever identity," a.k.a. the V (see *V*, below) a Changer ultimately selects after living as each of the four different assigned V's. A Mono cannot be the individual a Changer lived as during the approximately fourteen years before her/his Cycle (see *Cycle*, above) began.

RACHAS. Abbreviation of "Radical Changers," a small but growing splinter group of young Changers who seek not to live in secret, as the Council (see *Changers Council*, above) dictates. RaChas are freegans, anarchist free spirits, living in the margins, surviving on what human society at large throws away. RaChas philosophy calls for living openly as Changers and agitating for liberation and acceptance for all, Changers and Statics alike. RaChas have replaced their former emblem (an ancient Roman numeral IV rotated on its side) with a new image, a modified Changers emblem (see *Changers Emblem*, above) with multiple limbs (*Figure 3*), symbolizing the RaChas' desire to shake up traditional Changers philosophy and call attention to the limitations of the four-V Cycle (See *V*, below; see *Cycle*, above). RaChas have also been known to battle Abiders (see *Abider*, above) and even stage missions to rescue Changers who have been abducted by Abiders and held in Abider deprogramming camps. [*Nota bene*: while the Changers Council is at odds with the RaChas movement, it can also no longer deny its existence.]

FIG. 3. NEW RACHAS EMBLEM

STATIC. A non-Changer (i.e., the vast majority of the world's population). Particularly sympathetic Statics are ideal mates for Changers later in life. Once a Changer has completed his or her Cycle (see *Cycle*, above), s/he will be fully prepared to assess various Statics' openness and acceptance of difference. When a Changer feels certain that s/he has found an ideal potential Static mate, s/he may, with permission of the Council (see *Changers Council,* above), reveal her/himself to the Static. [*Nota bene:* This revelation can occur only after a Changer's full Cycle (see *Cycle*, above) is complete, and s/he has declared his or her Mono (see *Mono*, above).]

TOUCHSTONE. A Changer's official mentor, assigned immediately upon a Changer's transformation into her/his first V (see *V*, below). The same Touchstone is assigned for a Changer's entire Cycle (see *Cycle*, above).

V. Any one of a Changer's four versions of her/himself into which s/he changes during each of the four years of high school. Changers walk in the shoes of one V for each year (between the approximate ages of fourteen and eighteen).

Acknowledgments

Thanks are due to several individuals who helped *Changers* evolve from a lightning-bolt idea in the park to an actual book series we are proud to have our children (and others) read. The love, kindness, and support of the following friends, family, colleagues, and partners can be felt on every page of *Book Four* (and beyond):

Johnny Temple, Johanna Ingalls, Aaron Petrovich, Ibrahim Ahmad, and Susannah Lawrence at Akashic Books; Tana Jamieson and Mark Tuohy at A+E Studios; Kate Bornstein; Dixie and Matilda; our families; John Green; Ryan LeVine, Karl Austen, and Danielle Josephs at Jackoway, Tyerman, Wertheimer, et al.; Téa Leoni; A.J. Morewitz; Dawn Saltzman at Mosaic; Alex Petrowsky; Meryl Poster; Spencer Presler; Scott Turner Schofield; Zac Simmons at Paradigm; Doug Stewart at Sterling Lord Literistic; Tommy Wallach; Sarah Chalfant at the Wylie Agency.

And thank you especially to the readers who have stayed with us through four *Changers* installments.

ALLISON GLOCK-COOPER and **T COOPER** are best-selling and award-winning authors and journalists. Between them, they have published twelve books, raised two children, and rescued six dogs. The *Changers* series is their first collaboration in print. The two also write for television and film, and are currently adapting *Changers* for television. The authors can be reached via their websites: www.t-cooper.com and www.allisonglock.com.